YEAR OF CHANGE

To Shonda,
Happy Reading
TC Morris

TC MORRIS

outskirts press

A Year of Change

v4.0 r1.0

Outskirts Press, Inc.
http://www.outskirtspress.com

ISBN: 978-1-4787-9470-7

PRINTED IN THE UNITED STATES OF AMERICA

First and foremost, I would like to thank God for giving me the inspiration, courage, and persistence to make my dream a reality.

Thank you to my husband, children, family, and friends who supported me and helped critique my first adventure into the realm of author.

A special thank you to Jennette Remak for the invaluable advice given at the beginning of this project.

CHAPTER 1

As Cate Wilson, a young, widowed mother of two, stands huddled under the driveway shelter of Dr. Kimble's dental office with her two young girls, waiting for the rain to stop, she thinks, *The perfect end to another crappy day in the life of Cate Wilson. Two minutes late to work, and I get "The Eye" from Hector the Horrible. Then the car wouldn't start at lunchtime--had to have it towed to the shop; who knows what that will cost, or how I'm going to pay for it. Got a ride to daycare, then had to take the bus home with two kids. Get off the bus just in time for the skies to open up, and my umbrella is in the car. I'm exhausted and I still have to walk the three blocks home. Oh yeah, and the temperature is quickly dropping. According to Dr. Kimble's flashing sign, it's gone from 63° to 52° in the twenty minutes I've been standing here, and it's only October 17th. Thank goodness it's Friday.*

All of a sudden, Cate notices a car at the corner that seems to be having a problem, and the guy is getting out. Cate thinks, *Oh great, the cherry on top of this awesome day. Some guy's cute little convertible just flooded out at the corner and he's running this way. Now I have to figure out how to fight off a weirdo while holding on to two kids. Should have kept up with those kick-boxing classes.*

At the same time, Bill Sullivan, 36-year-old self-made billionaire and owner of Sullivan Enterprises, is driving his newly acquired classic little 1974 MG when he finds out it may not be as road-ready as he first thought. As the rain pours down, his windshield wipers seem to be slowing and he can barely see. He glances around to assess his options. *Oh man, this is a fine time for my windshield wipers to stop working--now I can't see a thing. What's going on? Oh no, don't die on me now. Great, okay—well, I don't want to sit in this car and just wait for someone to pile into to me. I'm gonna make a run for it to that doctor's office. Hopefully my phone is still working. Looks like someone else had to shelter there too.*

He reaches the shelter and is awe-struck by the woman huddled there with two little girls. He thinks, *Wow, she's beautiful, long auburn hair and those big green eyes. Holy cow--I think I'm in love.*

He shakes the rain from his thick black hair and it tumbles into his eyes. He smiles and says, "Hi, I'm Bill. This is some rain, huh? You broke down too? I'm calling a tow truck; I can tell them to send one of those big flat beds."

Cate looks at him warily and replies, "No, I rode the bus. We're just waiting for the rain to stop so we can walk home."

He glances up toward the sky and says, "It doesn't look like that's going to be anytime soon. I have a friend coming to get me; we can give you a ride, if you like."

Cate pulls her girls just a little bit closer and says, "No thank you. We're fine."

Kaylee, Cate's four-year-old, looks up at her mom and says, "Mommy, can we let him give us a ride? I'm hungry and getting cold."

Bill looks at the two little girls and thinks how much they look like their mom and hopes this beautiful woman is not married. "Look, I really don't mind. I'm sure you don't want to walk in this mess."

Cate looks down into Kaylee's little face and wrestles with her decision, but says, "No sir, thank you. I teach my daughters not to talk to strangers, so I surely can't set an example by taking a ride with one."

With disappointment, visible on his handsome face, he says, "Okay, suit yourself." He thinks, *Not sure if she's stuck up, or if she just thinks I'm some kind of weirdo.*

Cate takes another glance at the flashing sign and sees the temperature is now at 49°. She takes her jacket off and wraps it around Kaylee and digs the extra blanket out of the diaper bag for fifteen-month-old Shawn. The rain seems to be stopping and she can't wait to remove herself from this uncomfortable situation.

A few moments later, a big black pickup truck pulls up and a large burly guy gets out. Seeing him, Cate feels another jolt of anxiety. As he walks up, he smiles and nods toward her, then continues on to where Bill is standing. As Johnny, Bill's all-around go-to guy approaches, he gives it one more try. "Look, I'm not weird, or anything, I'm just trying to help. We would be glad to take you and your girls home."

Cate smiles politely and says, "No thanks, the rain is stopping; we'll be fine." She thinks, *There's no way in hell I would get into a truck with one strange man, let alone two. Especially not with my two babies.*

Bill really feels bad leaving them there, but doesn't want to come across like the weirdo she probably thinks he is, so he just says, "Okay, well, nice meeting you—umm, sorry, I didn't get your name."

She hesitates a moment, before answering, "Cate."

"Right, Cate." He turns to leave and says, "Okay, Johnny, let's go get the car taken care of."

Cate breathes a sigh of relief as they get into the truck and drive down to the street were his car is stalled. The rain has finally stopped, and she decides as soon as they get involved with his car, they're making a break for it before it starts raining again.

Once in the truck, Bill turns to Johnny and says, "See that girl I was talking to? I want you to find out who she is and why she has to take the bus with those two little girls."

Bill and Johnny have been friends since high school. When Johnny was shot in the line of duty as a police officer five years ago and couldn't return to full duty, Bill gave him a job as his driver/bodyguard/private detective, and anything-he-needs guy. Johnny is incredibly loyal, and Bill trusts him implicitly. Johnny takes a quick glance over his shoulder and says, "Sure, Boss, what's her name?"

"Cate."

"Cate what?"

"Just Cate."

Johnny laughs and shakes his head and says, "Great. This may take a while."

Bill, being a reasonable man, knows that's not much to go on, so he says, "No problem--you have 72 hours."

Cate lives in the same average middle-class neighborhood she grew up in, so normally she would feel perfectly safe walking the three blocks home, but after encountering two strange men, she walks home as quickly as possible. Once inside, she's relieved that they weren't followed. She locks the door behind them, takes a deep breath and sighs, "Thank God, we're finally home."

She tells Kaylee to go in the bathroom and take off her damp clothes. She puts some hotdogs to boil and quickly bathes the girls so they can get warm; then they sit down to eat.

By 9:00 both girls are fed, tucked in, and sleeping like two little angels. As Cate takes one more look at her babies snug in their little beds she thinks, *What a day. Time for me to take a nice hot soak and try to figure out what I'm going to do.*

After a warm bath and a good cry, and yet another bout of wondering how her life could go so wrong in just a year and a half, she finally crawls into her bed, closes her eyes, and thinks, *Oh Sean, why did you have to leave us?*

CHAPTER 2

At 4:20 a.m., Cate wakes with a start from a crazy dream about the guy in the rain. This time she's alone under the shelter, he comes running up all wet and sexy, with that gorgeous black hair falling into those piercing blue bedroom eyes. Not saying a word; he just walks up to her and starts kissing her real tender and slow. She shakes her head and says aloud, "What the hell is wrong with me? As if someone like him would want someone like me, a total mess with two babies. Besides, I don't want another man. After Sean, I could never love like that again, and you don't get that twice in one lifetime."

She gets up, knowing there's no going back to sleep now, and tries to figure out which bills she can pay this week. She decides with this early start she can also get the laundry done before they leave to visit her mom at the rehab center.

By 10:30, Cate has paid her bills online, cleaned the house, washed and folded two loads of laundry, fed the girls and has them loaded in her mother's car, and is on the way to Diamond Cove Rehab Center.

Thirty minutes later, she unbuckles the girls from their car seats and grabs a few toys for them to bring in, she tells them, "Come on, girls, let's go see Grandma." Cate feels bad that she can visit her mom only on weekends.

They go straight to her mother's room, but she's not in there. Cate, being the worrier she is, naturally thinks the worst and rushes to the nurse's station. There she sees Regina, a young nurse that usually works Saturdays. Fighting back the urge to panic, she says, "Regina, I'm looking for my mother. She's not in her room--do you know where she is?"

Regina looks up and smiles. "Sure--Phoebe's in therapy this morning. She should be done in about ten minutes. You can wait in her room. I'll let her know you're here."

Breathing a little sigh of relief, Cate returns to her mom's room and takes out the toys to keep the girls occupied. Twenty minutes later, her mom returns from therapy and is happy to see them waiting for her. "Hi, Cate--oh, there's my little angels." Kaylee runs to her grandmother and Shawn's little face lights up.

Phoebe had a stroke three months ago and has been in Diamond Cove Rehab Center for the last two and a half months since being released from the hospital. She's been working hard to get back on her feet and making progress, but it's a slow process.

As the girls run to their grandmother, Cate smiles. "Hi, Mom. We got here a little early today. Wow, you're really putting in the hours. I'm surprised they had therapy on Saturday morning."

Phoebe chuckles. "Well, I sweet-talked my physical therapist, Donnie, into giving me an extra session since he was working this weekend anyway. Is everything okay? You look beat. What's going on?"

Her mother knows her so well. Cate starts the recap of her week and finally gets to the events of yesterday, explaining, "My car died yesterday, I had to have it towed to Bobby's shop. He said he would only charge me for the parts, but still that's $250. I told him I wanted to pay for his labor too, but he said no way, it was the least he could do. He reminded me that Sean was his best friend and he would do the same if the situation was reversed. It will be a couple more weeks until I can get the money, so I'll have to use your car until then."

"No problem; it's not like I'm using it right now. I hope I'll be able to drive again one day, but until then you gotta keep it running for me. That was some storm last night. Did you get caught in it?"

Cate rolls her eyes. "Yeah, we had to take the bus home from daycare and had to wait out the rain in front of Dr. Kimble's office. I was a little scared when this guy came running up to us, but it was okay--his car broke down at the corner. He seemed nice, even offered to give us a ride home, but I turned him down. Of course, I had second thoughts after the first block, because Shawn's getting so heavy and Kaylee was tired and cold by then."

Cate and Phoebe continue catching each other up on the week's events. Soon they realize it's already lunch time, so they head to the cafeteria. As Cate wheels her mom with both girls on her lap, she thinks, *It's so good to hang out with Mom. I miss her being home with me every day. I'm just so glad she's making such good progress. I don't know what I would have done if she had left us, too. I can't wait until she's able to come home.*

After lunch, they spend the rest of the afternoon talking and playing games with the girls. Phoebe and Cate have always been close and enjoy each other's company. Even when Cate was growing up, they seemed to have found a way to avoid the usual teenage conflict between mother and daughter.

After Cate's dad, Frank, died five years ago of a sudden heart attack while jogging, she and her mother seemed to get even closer. Then when Sean died, she just couldn't bring herself to stay in their house alone, so she moved back in with her mom. Back to the same room she grew up in.

By 3:00 the girls are restless, so as much as Cate hates it, it's time to go home. She hugs and kisses her mother goodbye and promises to bring some homemade cookies the next day. Phoebe hates for them to leave, but after a thorough workout at physical therapy that morning, she's tired.

For the last three months, Cate's life has been a hectic mess. Most days she feels like a hamster on an exercise wheel. Get up at 5:30, shower and get ready for work before getting the girls fed, dressed and off to daycare, go to work, pick the girls up from daycare, go home, fix dinner, squeeze in a little play time before bathing the girls and getting them to bed, clean the kitchen, then collapse into bed herself by 10:30, if she's lucky. Weekends are spent cleaning the house, doing laundry, grocery shopping, and visiting her mom. She can barely remember what life used to be like before Sean's death.

CHAPTER 3

For the last three days, Bill hasn't been able to stop thinking about the beautiful "Cate," and can wait no longer to find out whether she's married. He picks up his desk phone and punches in Johnny's number. Johnny doesn't have set hours; he's on call for Bill 24/7. He answers on the second ring and Bill skips the formalities and gets right to the point.

"Hey, Johnny, it's Tuesday morning. You got some information for me?"

Although it's only 7:00, Johnny's never surprised to hear from Bill early in the morning. Bill has always been an early riser and often calls before breakfast to give him tasks he needs carried out each day. Johnny's known Bill long enough to know he's a man of action and when his mind is set on something, he's relentless.

"Hey, boss, you weren't kidding about the 72 hours, huh?"

Bill just says, "You know me."

Johnny quickly realizes his boss doesn't want to make small talk, so he jumps right into it. "Okay, well--Cate is Catherine Wilson, age twenty-seven, widowed. Her husband Sean Wilson was a Marine. He was killed by an IED in Afghanistan a year and a half ago. They had one little girl, Kaylee, and Cate was six months pregnant with the second child at the time."

"After the second child was born, another girl, Shawn--I guess named after her husband--Cate sells their home and moves in with her mother. It looks like she socked away the profit from the sale of the house, not much, about 10k, but in the past few months has been dipping into it pretty regular.

"Cate is the office manager for a mid-sized printing firm called Sunrise Printing. They do mainly business promotional items. She's been there six years, started right out of college.

"Her mother, Phoebe Carter, had a stoke three months ago. She's in Diamond Cove Rehab Facility. Up until then, her mother watched the two girls while Cate worked. Cate now has them in daycare and it looks like she's been contributing to the cost of the rehab center that the insurance doesn't cover. Seems she's pretty strapped for funds--her 10k is now right around 2k.

"Looks like the reason she was riding the bus is her car broke down Friday and was towed to a repair shop. Let's see... what's the name? Oh yeah, here it is, Bobby's Auto Repair on 6th Avenue. That's about all I got, boss. Is this enough, or should I dig deeper?"

Bill thinks for a minute, then replies, "Yeah, yeah, that's enough for now on her, but find out all you can about this Sunrise Printing and get back to me." Bill hangs up without waiting for a reply.

Johnny answers, "Sure, will do," but realizes Bill's already gone. He knows Bill wasn't being rude; he's always this way when he's preoccupied.

After hanging up with Johnny, Bill sits at his desk tapping his pen, contemplating how he wants to proceed, then reaches for the phone again. This time he calls Laura, his assistant. "Laura, would you get me Ben Donaldson?"

Laura's worked with Bill for the past ten years and is much more to Bill than the title "assistant" covers; she's more like a second mother to him. Less than three minutes later, she has Ben Donaldson on the line and puts him through to Bill.

Ben Donaldson is a nationally renowned neurologist. He and Bill's older brother, TJ, went to medical school together, and he's been a great family friend ever since. Ben, Bill, and TJ get together every couple of months for a Sunday of golf, so it's not out of the ordinary for Bill to call him.

"Hi, Ben--it's Bill Sullivan. How are you?"

"I'm great, man. It's good to hear from you. You looking to beat me at golf again?"

Bill laughs, because it's usually Ben that beats both him and TJ. "Well, I do really enjoy that, but today I'm calling you on professional business."

Ben's a little surprised, but says, "Sure, what's up?"

Bill puts his pen down on the desk and sits up a little straighter. "Tell me what you know about Diamond Cove Rehab."

"It's a good facility; some of my patients go there. Good staff, not the most expensive, but certainly not the cheapest. Why, what's going on?"

"Do you have access to their records?"

"Yeah, in fact I have a patient that checked in there last week."

"Can you check on one of their other patients and let me know her prognosis?"

Ben, now a little concerned, asks if this patient is family.

Bill senses that Ben may be uncomfortable giving out too much information, so he lies just a little. "No, the mother of a friend --she had a stroke about three months ago. I know they're a little strapped for cash, so I just wanted to see what's going on, so maybe I could help."

Ben relaxes a bit; he knows Bill is a good guy and is always helping people in need. That's one of the reasons he has such loyal employees. "What's the name?"

"Phoebe Carter."

Ben accesses the files for Diamond Cove and starts searching. "Carter, Phoebe, here she is. Looks like she's progressing well. She probably has another few months of treatment ahead."

"Is her doctor any good?"

"Dr. Tibbs? Yes, he's a good doctor and a good guy. Not me, of course, but good."

Bill hesitates only a second, takes a deep breath and says, "Okay, this is what I'd like you to do. Get Mrs. Carter into one of your case studies and I'll pay all the cost."

Ben is a little taken aback. "Bill, case studies don't cost the patient anything, but I don't have anything going on right now."

"Sure you do, and I'm funding it. Phoebe Carter is your case. Get her what's needed, rehabbed and out quick. I'll cover all the cost for you and the facility. Just tell everyone you are selecting one patient from each facility and she meets the criteria."

"Wow, this must be some friend. It's going to take a little arranging, but I'll start working on it tomorrow. You know this is going to be expensive, right?"

Bill laughs a little and says, "That's okay--I think I can cover it."

Ben laughs too. "I know you can. I'll update you as soon as I get this worked out."

They disconnect, and Bill picks up the phone again. "Laura, I want to pay for the repairs of someone's car at Bobby's Auto Repair--anonymously, of course. Would you take care of this for me?"

Laura, like Ben, knows this is something Bill does for people. Sometimes an employee, other times a complete stranger that he heard needs help through a news story, so she just says, "Sure, what's the name?"

"Cate Wilson. Tell them to make it a priority, and let me know when it's taken care of. Thanks, Laura; you're the best."

Laura just smiles and shakes her head as she hangs up.

When Bill hangs up the phone, he kicks back in his chair again and thinks, *Well, Cate Wilson, with the beautiful big green eyes, I hope this eases your burden a little.*

CHAPTER 4

Cate has been wrestling for the past week and a half with how she's going to juggle the bills, pay for her car repairs, and the $1500 due next month for her mother's care at Diamond Cove. After a morning full of meetings, phone calls, and her boss, Hector's snide remarks, she finally sits down at her desk to eat the yogurt and apple she brought for lunch. She decides it's time to bite the bullet and call Diamond Cove to talk to Mrs. Romanoff, the director, about making some type of payment arrangements. She picks up the phone, bites her lip and dials the number.

"Mrs. Romanoff, this is Cate Wilson. I know my mom's bill for next month is coming due soon, but I don't have the full $1500 right now, I have some unexpected repairs on my car, but as soon as I get it out of the shop I'm going to sell it and that should cover a few more months."

Mrs. Romanoff, is a little surprised by the phone call and says, "Ms. Wilson, didn't your mother call you? Just this morning we found out that she's been chosen to participate in a case study of stroke recovery procedures by the renowned neurologist Dr. Ben Donaldson. All her future care and the facility fees will be covered by the foundation conducting the study. Maybe your mother didn't fully understand how this works."

Cate is stunned and can't comprehend what she's hearing. "What? When? I don't understand. How did this happen?"

"Well, Dr. Donaldson's office called, and they were choosing one patient from each rehab facility for a case study and your mother fit their criteria. They brought all the paperwork over this morning and your mother signed up. I'm surprised she didn't call you."

Cate grabs her cell phone out of her purse and sees three missed calls from her mom. "I've been in meetings all morning. I just can't believe this--I don't know what to say. I've been praying so hard for help. This is incredible. Thank you." As she hangs up with Mrs. Romanoff, she thinks, *Darn, I should have checked my cell before calling Mrs. Romanoff.*

Cate's hands are shaking as she calls her mother's room. "Mom, I just spoke to Mrs. Romanoff. She tells me you were selected for a case study by a Dr. Donaldson."

When Phoebe answers the phone she's even more excited than Cate, if that's possible. "Yes. Cate, I was so shocked. I've heard of this doctor before, and I've asked some of the nurses about him. Everyone tells me he's the best and how lucky I am."

Cate now has tears running down her cheeks as she hears the excitement in her mother's voice. "Oh Mom, I was calling Mrs. Romanoff to try to make payment arrangements for next month and she told me that all expenses will be covered by the foundation conducting the study. I just can't believe this--our prayers are being answered. I'm going to stop at church this evening to light a candle and say a prayer of thanks to God for this blessing."

Phoebe hears the tears in her daughter's voice and starts to cry herself. "Please light one for me too. I'm going to meet with Dr. Donaldson at 9:00 tomorrow. Can you come?"

Without a moment's hesitation she says, "Yes, definitely. I'll let Hector know I'll be late tomorrow." When she hangs up the phone, she sits at her desk and cries tears of relief for the next five minutes before she can pull herself together.

Cate heads to Hector's office to explain why she'll be late to work the next day. He can see she's been crying, and in a rare moment of compassion, is supportive, telling her to take as long as she needs.

The next morning Cate is so excited, she arrives at Diamond Cove twenty minutes early, she and Phoebe sit in her room, still trying to comprehend how this could happen when Dr. Donaldson walks in, right on time.

Ben has been studying Phoebe's charts and going over how he wants to proceed with her treatment, before meeting his new patient and making any final decisions.

"Hi, Mrs. Carter. I'm Dr. Donaldson."

Phoebe is all smiles as she shakes Ben's hand. "Hi, Dr. Donaldson; it's so nice to meet you. This is my daughter, Cate Wilson. I asked her to come. I hope that's okay."

Ben extends his hand to Cate and says, "Of course, we encourage family participation and support." As he looks at Cate, he quickly realizes why Bill is so anxious to help this lady. Ben turns his attention to Phoebe and continues, "As you know, this is part of a case study, so it's going to be strict and probably a lot of hard work on your part, Phoebe. Are you ready for that?"

"You bet. I've been trying to get into therapy twice a day, but they don't have space for me. So, I only get in once daily, but I do my exercises in my room all throughout the day."

"That's great. I think you'll see remarkable progress with our program."

Cate is still confused about how this all came about, so she asks, "Doctor, how did you come to choose my mother for this program?"

Sticking with the story, Ben replies, "Well, I had my staff screen all the stoke patients from the five rehab facilities in the area. We only selected one patient per facility and after receiving all the charts from this one, we felt Phoebe was the best fit for our study." He doesn't want Cate asking too many questions, so he turns his attention back to Phoebe.

"Now Phoebe, I would like to give you a thorough exam before I prescribe any treatment. I've already consulted with Dr. Tibbs, and he agreed this would be a good opportunity for you. He also told me how determined you are to make a full recovery. So, I would like to get started right away and unless either of you has any more questions, we'll get you to the examining room now. Ms. Wilson, you are welcome to wait if you like, but unfortunately, I don't allow anyone in the examining room with the patients."

Cate does have more questions, but doesn't want to delay her mom getting started, so she says, "No, that's okay. I really have to get to work. Mom, I'll call you tonight. I love you. Dr. Donaldson, thank you again for this opportunity."

CHAPTER 5

After examining Phoebe and reviewing her files over the next few days, Ben Donaldson is excited to get this treatment started, so he picks up his phone and dials Bill.

"Hi, Bill. I just wanted to check in with you on Phoebe Carter's treatment. By the way, I wanted to thank you, too. This lady is a dream patient, and she's very excited. I examined her and spent several hours going over my treatment protocol with her and she didn't even blink an eye at the hours of hard work I explained she has ahead. I love treating patients that aren't moping and feeling sorry for themselves."

"That's great, Ben. What's it look like?"

"Well, you said you want her out as quickly as possible, so I'm going to be aggressive with my treatment. I want to get her into hyperbaric oxygen therapy daily for the next three weeks, along with an adjusted more advanced physical therapy program. I wanted to run it by you first, because this won't be cheap. I'm thinking with three weeks of hyperbaric and the extended PT my fees and the facility fees you're looking at a couple hundred thousand over the next month or so. But I think she may be able to go home by then. The follow-up treatment will just depend on how all this goes."

Without hesitation Bill says, "Okay, let's do it."

Ben knew the money wouldn't be an issue, but he smiles and says, "Bill, I met her daughter. I can see why you are so motivated to help, but do you know this girl well enough to put out this kind of money?"

Bill laughs and says, "Ben, I don't know her at all, yet. Keep me posted on her progress." He breaks off the connection.

After hanging up with Ben, he dials Johnny to see what he's got on Sunrise Printing. Johnny answers on the second ring, as usual, and Bill jumps right to the point. "Johnny, give me an update on this printing company."

Johnny has all his notes ready; he's been expecting Bill's call. "Well, as I told you, they are a mid-sized company clearing about three million a year. They've been in business for forty-three years, started and still owned by Chuck Lawden. They started out printing business forms and flyers but have evolved into mostly banners, signs, and graphic design.

"Lawden is semi-retired, but still has final say. He has a VP named Hector Gonzales, who has been with him for sixteen years. Gonzales runs the day-to-day operations. Your girl Cate is the office manager; she's been there six years. They also have four graphic artists, four warehouse guys and a receptionist. So, eleven employees in all. Lawden's turning a pretty good profit."

This is better news than Bill expected. The wheels are turning as he says, "Okay, thanks. I'll talk to you later."

With his mind racing, he calls Laura and asks her to have Ed Clancy come to his office.

A few minutes later, Ed Clancy, the head of Sullivan Enterprises' legal department, enters Bill's office. Ed, like Laura, has been with Sullivan Enterprises for the last ten years, since the beginning.

Bill started a small technology development firm while still in college and five years later sold some groundbreaking programs to one of the largest tech companies in the country. Sullivan Enterprises is still heavy in the technology field, but Bill thought it smart to diversify and started buying out small to mid-sized businesses in different fields. So far, every business he's acquired has been successful and profitable.

"Ed, I want you to do an analysis on a company called Sunrise Printing. Find out if the owner Chuck Lawden is interested in selling and see what we can get it for."

Ed's a little confused, but he's been through all the previous acquisitions with Bill, so he knows how fast Bill's mind works. "Sure, Bill. Are we expanding into the printing business now?"

Smiling, Bill replies, "I think it's a very good possibility."

CHAPTER 6

It's been a few days since Cate got the news about her mom getting into the case study, and as she sits at her desk, she thinks that she just might start to have a little breathing room when her phone rings. She answers, "Good morning, Cate Wilson, may I help you?"

She immediately recognizes the voice on the other end. "Hi, Cate--it's Bobby. Just wanted to let you know your car's ready."

"What? I told you not to start on it until I had the money, and that wouldn't be for a few weeks."

Bobby says, "Don't worry, it's paid for. Some lady came in a last week and said she was dropping off the payment for you and to just let you know when it was ready."

Cate is stunned and almost drops the phone. "What lady? What was her name?"

"I don't know. I wasn't here when she came in. One of my guys took the payment. She paid in cash is all I know. So, if you want, Sue and I can drop your car off to you this evening."

Cate doesn't know what to say. She manages to get out, "Yeah, sure, but that is so weird. Ask the guys to describe her to you so I can try to figure out who it is and why she would do this."

Bobby was a childhood friend of Cate's husband Sean and knows how tough things have been for her. He says,

"Look, kid, maybe you shouldn't look a gift horse in the mouth and just accept it as your luck finally changing. See you this evening."

Later that evening, Bobby and his wife Sue drop her car off, and he tells her that not only did this mystery lady pay for the repairs, but also paid for new tires, a tune-up, new hoses, and belts, and insisted the full price of the labor be added in. All totaling $2700.

Cate is still having trouble comprehending it all and wonders what is going on. Who is this woman?

She keeps going over in her mind what Bobby said. From his guy's description, this lady was in her late fifties, or early sixties, average height, very well dressed, dark hair, and wore glasses. Well, that fits about a million or so women including her Aunt Alison, Phoebe's sister. She immediately calls her aunt, but Alison insists she doesn't know anything about it. She explains that she really doesn't have a spare $2700 just lying around, and if she did, she would have to put it into her own car. Cate knows that's true.

They have such a small family; it's just Phoebe, Cate, and Aunt Alison, Uncle Kirk, and their two kids, Brent and Brenda. She just can't imagine who this could be.

She wonders if maybe Bobby's right--it's like winning the lottery. You don't wonder why; you just take it gratefully and thank God for the blessing. Maybe her luck is starting to change.

Cate reflects over the last year and a half since Sean's death and thinks, *The only good thing to happen to me was little Shawn, and I cried when she was born too, because she and Kaylee would never know how great their dad was.* Suddenly she thinks, *Wait, that's it. It had to be Sean's mom and dad. Why didn't I think of them before?*

She calls them right away, but after hanging up with Pat and Debbie she's still as clueless as before. Though they said they would have gladly chipped in for the repairs, they didn't even know her car was broken. Which is true--she hasn't spoken to them in about three weeks.

She wishes they lived closer. Pat and Debbie only get to see the girls about once a month when they take turns driving the three hours to visit one another, and they've made the trip the last two months since Phoebe's stroke.

She just can't think of anyone else and shrugs, thinking, *Well, sooner or later I guess I'll find out, but now I have to work on Kaylee's Halloween costume for tomorrow night.* She's grateful that Kaylee wants to be a ghost; that's an easy one, and Shawn can wear Kaylee's old pumpkin costume.

CHAPTER 7

Over the next three weeks, Phoebe makes remarkable progress, thanks to her new treatment regime. Now it's two days before Thanksgiving, and Phoebe is coming home. Cate's so excited; it's been lonely in the house without her. They've always been close, but since Sean's death, Phoebe has really been her rock. Cate knows she couldn't have survived without her.

As she drives to Diamond Cove Rehab, she reflects on that horrible day last July, when they were at the park with the girls and her mom said she had such a bad headache. As they packed up to leave, she said she couldn't walk, and her face and arm on the left side were just drooping. Phoebe had to go by ambulance to the hospital. The doctors said it was a good thing they got her there so quickly--that it really helped minimize the long-term effects.

Now after four long months, her mom is finally coming home. Cate thinks of what a blessing Dr. Donaldson has been. Of course, Phoebe will still need a cane to walk and will still have some limitations, but at least she'll be home for the holidays. She glances toward the sky and knows they truly have a lot to be thankful for.

By the time they get home and settle in with the list of instructions, medications, and the weekly continuing physical therapy schedule, it's time to pick up the girls from daycare. Cate insists that their neighbor Beth, the seventeen-year-old who occasionally babysits for Kaylee and Shawn, stay with Phoebe while she goes to pick up the girls. Of course, Phoebe thinks it's unnecessary, but agrees to make Cate feel better. As she leaves, she tells Beth to not let her mom do too much; she doesn't want her overdoing things.

Cate is thankful that through this case study, they supply the medications and transportation to and from therapy. She says a silent prayer of thanks again for Dr. Donaldson picking Phoebe for this study.

When they get home, the girls are so happy that their grandma is there waiting for them. Kaylee chatters on non-stop, and Shawn has decided she has to bring all her toys out to play with Grandma. Shawn is all smiles as she stumbles back and forth with her treasures. When Phoebe went into the hospital, Shawn still needed help walking.

Thanksgiving will be at Aunt Alison's house this year. This was supposed to be their year to host, but Alison volunteered and insisted she would take care of all the food. Another blessing.

While things are improving, Cate also knows the struggle is not over, her job has been pretty hectic lately and of course Hector, being his usual charming self, always has to make little comments about her leaving work at the normal 5:00 quitting time. Before her mom's stroke, she would stay until 5:30 or 6:00, but her mom would have the girls and dinner would be ready when she got home. Now the girls are in daycare, and she has to leave by 5:00 to pick them up.

Even though Phoebe's home now, she still can't watch the girls, not yet, so Cate decides Hector will just have to deal with it. She doesn't see what the big deal is anyway; all her work is getting done. She usually works through lunch to make sure of it. Cate shakes her head and thinks, *Hector's just a jerk. Things were much better when Mr. Lawden was in the office every day.*

CHAPTER 8

Ed Clancy has been in negotiations with Chuck Lawden for a few weeks now and calls Bill to give him the weekly update.

"Bill, it's Ed. The negotiations with Sunrise are going well; Lawden's very excited by your offer. He says being semi-retired for the past couple of years has been nice, but he is really looking forward to making it full time."

Bill is really getting excited about this now and asks, "When do you think we can actually close the deal?"

Ed's feeling good about the path the negotiations have taken and thinks they can close by the end of the year, for sure. He informs Bill that Mr. Lawden would like to have a face-to-face with him before they sign any final papers. He's concerned about his employees and wants to make sure Bill isn't going to go in and clean house. All his employees have been with him for a while, and he's concerned about their welfare.

Bill agrees that's a good idea and tells Ed to set up a meeting for the following week and to let Laura know when he has the date and time, so she can put it on his calendar.

Bill has had Johnny keeping tabs on Cate and calls him for an update as well, "Johnny, what's the latest on Cate Wilson?"

"Well, boss, looks like things are getting better for Ms. Wilson. Her mother was sent home from the rehab center, which of course you know. She's pretty strapped financially, though. Looks like everything she makes goes into daycare and the household bills. Before she got sick, Ms. Carter used to work evenings and weekends as an assistant manager at Starbucks, so she's lost that income. Now she only gets her husband's social security and her disability, which ain't enough to live comfortably on, but it looks like they're makin' it, but not much extra."

As much as he would like to sweep in and make everything great for her, he knows he can't, so he tells Johnny he's meeting with Chuck Lawden next week to talk about this buy-out and wants him to start doing some research on all the other employees to see if there would be enough need for an onsite daycare.

Johnny's not sure he likes where this is heading, but says, "Sure, will do."

As Bill hangs up the phone, he says aloud, "Cate Wilson, what the hell have you done to me? I've never been so attracted to a woman that wouldn't even talk to me. Now you've got me buying a company, just so I can get close to you."

The following week as they leave their meeting with Chuck Lawden, Bill tells Ed, "I think that meeting went really well. I like Lawden; he's a hard-working, honest man. I respect him for caring so much about his employees. He reminds me a little of my dad."

Ed agrees, "Yeah, he liked you too. He told me he got a good feeling about you and he appreciated that you took the time to learn about each of his employees and even knew their names. We agreed to close in two weeks, on December 29th. He asked if you would go with him after the closing to break the news to the employees and have you put their minds at ease about their future employment."

Bill thinks that's a great idea. He decides he'll have Laura order in lunch for everyone. As his mind races, he says, "The closing is at 8:00, so ask Lawden to have a meeting arranged with all the employees for 11:00. That'll give us an hour to make the announcement and answer their questions. We'll break for lunch; then I can meet with everyone one-on-one for the rest of the afternoon. Have we gotten all the information to HR?"

Ed nods. "Yep, sent everything over already. We'll just need everyone to sign their offer letters by the 31st, and we'll be good to go for January 1st."

"You got all the benefits information for them?"

"Yeah, boss, I got it. Why are you so nervous about this deal? This is small potatoes compared to our usual acquisitions."

Bill shakes his head. "Good question. I just feel like there's a lot at stake for me this time, and I want to do this right."

CHAPTER 9

It's December 29th and all Cate can think as she drives to work is *Thank goodness, it's Friday and I don't have to come back to work until Tuesday.* It's been a rough week with trying to close out the year, and this morning she's running late again. As she pulls into the parking lot she glances at the time on the dashboard and says to herself, *Great, ten minutes late. I can't believe I caught the bridge two days in a row--Hector will never believe it. Last thing I need is to have to deal with him this morning. Well, here goes.*

She takes a deep breath as she walks in the door and hurries past Hector's office. As she sets her purse down she thinks, *Wow. He didn't even look up from his desk when I passed. Maybe he didn't notice I was late.* But then she hears him coming out of his office and sighs. *Uh-oh, I spoke too soon. Here he comes.*

Hector pokes his head into her office and says, "Cate, I need you to let everyone know we have a staff meeting at 11:00. Mr. Lawden just called and said he wants everyone there, no exceptions."

"Sure. What's going on?"

"I don't know, but I have a bad feeling about this." As he walks away he adds, "By the way, you were ten minutes late. What, the bridge up again, or was it the train this time?"

Ugh! He's such a jerk.

By 11:00 everyone's a little on edge and nervous as they all file into the meeting room. All morning, everyone's been speculating on what this is all about. Cate keeps praying that Mr. Lawden isn't closing the business. She can't imagine what she would do if that happened. She's one of the last to enter the meeting room, because she was on a call with a customer, so she takes a seat at the back of the room. As soon as she sits down she hears Mr. Lawden enter the building talking to someone.

She closes her eyes, takes a deep breath and thinks, *Here we go; time for the bombshell.*

Mr. Lawden enters the meeting room with two other men in suits. Now everyone really starts to get antsy, looking at one another as the men settle at the head of the long table. Cate sits up a little taller trying to get a better look at the two strangers. She thinks, *That one guy looks so familiar. Where have I met him before? He's really good-looking, and wow, those blue eyes look right through you.* As recognition sets in, she starts to pale. *Oh no, it can't be, that's the guy in the rain.* She's sure of it, but why on earth is he here?

Mr. Lawden has always been so cheerful, but this morning he looks very serious. Could her worst fears be coming true? Mr. Lawden looks around the room and begins, "Good morning, everyone. I know you are all probably wondering what this is all about. Well, I'll get right to it, I'm retiring, full time, and I've sold the business."

Everyone in the room gasps. Cate feels her heart sink.

Mr. Lawden raises his hands, realizing he may have been a little too blunt. "Now, now--before you go getting all flustered, let me explain. Mr. Sullivan here owns Sullivan Enterprises and has made me a very generous offer. He wants to add Sunrise Printing to his portfolio, and after a lot of negotiating and soul-searching, I've decided to take his offer. It's what I think is best for me, Sunrise, and all of you. I know you probably have a thousand questions running through your minds right now, so I'm going to let Mr. Sullivan introduce himself, and then we'll answer all your questions."

From the moment Bill entered the room, he was searching for that beautiful face. It took less than three seconds for him to spot her sitting in the very back of the room. As he steps up, he has to make a mental effort not to stare at the stunning Ms. Cate Wilson.

He clears his throat and begins. "Hi, I'm Bill Sullivan, as Mr. Lawden said, I own Sullivan Enterprises, which encompasses thirteen different companies under the Sullivan Enterprises umbrella, and we have a lot of printing and graphic needs across the board. I believe adding a printing business to the fold would more than pay for itself in the savings on our printing costs alone. I became interested in Sunrise because it has been a solid business for many years with a very good reputation. I want to reassure everyone that you don't have to worry about your jobs. You folks know the printing business, and I will depend on you to make this profitable for all of us.

"Mr. Lawden has very high praise for this entire team, and I trust his judgment. We've prepared a packet for each of you to introduce you to Sullivan Enterprises. I know you have a lot of questions, so we'll start taking your questions, then we're having lunch brought in for everyone. After lunch, I would like to meet briefly with each of you to discuss your future with the Sullivan family of businesses. Okay, let's get started. First question."

He makes sure to look at every person individually as he speaks to them, even though he really wants to fix his gaze on Cate and examine every inch of her exquisite face.

Everyone starts asking questions, but Cate can't even understand what they're saying. She feels like she's frozen. All that keeps going through her mind is *Why does he keep glancing my way? Oh God, I hope he doesn't remember me*. As she replays in her mind their last meeting, she remembers she wasn't very nice to him that day in the rain. He even offered her a ride home and she refused because she thought he was a weirdo. She keeps thinking, *Oh no, I think I'm going to faint.*

Finally, the chance she's been looking for--the food arrives, and she hurries out of the meeting room to show the delivery person where to bring the food. She grabs a bottle of water and holds it to her head. The cold helps to calm her, so she can think. As she starts to regain her composure she thinks, *Okay Cate, pull it together, eat a little lunch, drink some water, take a few deep breaths, and put your professional face on. A guy like that probably doesn't remember a stupid little chance encounter anyway.*

She can hear that things are starting to wrap up in the meeting room, so she grabs a turkey sandwich and her water and goes to her office. Luckily, Mr. Sullivan is still busy talking to everyone as they enter the lunch room, so she sits at her desk and takes a bite of her sandwich--not really sure if she can actually swallow it--and starts going through her email. Just as she starts to feel like she can breathe again, there's a soft knock on her door, and there he is.

"Ms. Wilson, is this a good time to meet with you?"

She's not sure if she physically jumped when he knocked, or not, but tries to cover, saying, "Oh, yes. Sure. I was just answering some emails."

As Bill and the other man enter her office, she feels her chest tighten again. He's nervous too, but being the professional negotiator, he is, he knows how to be calm on the outside, so you never know what he's thinking.

"This is Ed Clancy, the head of our legal department. He has our introduction and benefits package for you, and there's an offer letter for you to review and sign, if you choose to stay with Sullivan Enterprises, which I really hope you do."

All she can say is, "Oh, okay."

Ed steps into her office and hands her a Sullivan Enterprises folder, "Here you go, Ms. Wilson. You can take a couple of days to look everything over, and if you have any questions, the number for our HR department is right there on the front of the package. We will need your acceptance by the 31st--I know that's Sunday, but we will need it signed and emailed in so we can have everyone entered in the system for January 1st." Ed feels like he's intruding on a private moment, so he excuses himself, saying, "I'll leave you two to your meeting now."

Cate opens the packet; so she doesn't have to look into those eyes, she says, "Wow, this is all so overwhelming. I truly wasn't expecting anything like this when I woke up this morning."

Bill smiles and sits in the chair across the desk from her. "I understand. I know this is all a whirlwind, but I just want everyone to know that I will be working closely with you and Hector to make this transition as smooth as possible. I noticed you didn't have any questions earlier, I'd be glad to answer any that you have now."

Her mind can only focus on one word. *He's going to be working "closely" with us--how "closely"?* Cate can't understand why she's so rattled by this man.

She does her best to keep her hands from shaking. "Well, I guess I was a little in shock, and everyone else was doing a pretty good job of covering the same things that immediately came to my mind. I'm sure once I have a chance to absorb all of this, I will have more questions."

Bill smiles; he can see how nervous she is. "Good. Like Ed said, the offer letter and the benefits package are all right there. You can call HR--someone will be available all weekend--or me, if you need anything. Here's my card with my cell number. I'll be glad to address any concerns you have. For now, I'd like to go over what you are currently doing and explain my vision for the future."

Cate finally starts to relax as she explains her duties to him. He sees the change as she starts to talk about her work, so he asks questions not only about her job, but the business as a whole. He quickly realizes that she is not just a pretty face; this woman knows this business and will be a very valuable asset to its growth.

CHAPTER 10

As Cate drives home that evening, she's still so amazed at the events of the day. What a way to end the year--when she left for work this morning, the last thing on her mind was that she would be working for a different company by the end of the day, and to think her new boss would be the one person she thought she might have to fight off to protect herself and her kids! Wow, what a turn of events.

When Cate walks in the door, her mom calls out from the kitchen, and both girls run to see Grandma. Cate's so grateful to have her mom back home and getting back to her old self. She follows the girls into the kitchen and is relieved that Phoebe has supper ready.

She tells Kaylee to go wash up and picks up Shawn to wash her face and hands while Phoebe starts fixing the girls' plates. As they sit down to eat, Phoebe asks Cate how her day was.

Cate chuckles. "Mom, you won't believe the day I had. I thought today was going to be another bad day, especially after catching the bridge again. But when I got to work, Hector came in right away saying we had a big staff meeting at 11. Well, the big news was that Mr. Lawden is retiring, and he sold the business."

"Oh Cate, no! Please don't tell me you're losing your job."

"No. Not at all. He sold the business to Sullivan Enterprises and the owner, Bill Sullivan, was there with him. He assured everyone that their jobs were secure. They passed out the benefits package and offer letters to everyone and we have until the 31st to accept the offer or resign."

"Wow. Do you think anyone will be resigning?"

"I don't think so. Everyone was pretty excited with the offers. The benefits are much better than we currently have, and I don't know about anyone else, but my salary offer includes a 10% raise."

"Oh Cate, that's wonderful. What do you think of this new owner?"

"Well, that the craziest part. Do you remember that day a couple of months ago when my car broke down and I had to catch the bus home? Remember I told you we had to wait out that rainstorm in front of Dr. Kimble's office?"

"Yeah. I kind of remember you telling me about that."

"Remember, I told you I thought I would have to fight off some weird guy whose car stalled at the corner and he offered me a ride home when his friend got there to pick him up? Well, the weird guy is my new boss."

"Oh no. Are you sure?"

"Oh yes, I'm sure."

"Did he remember you?"

"I don't think so. If he did, he didn't mention anything. Thank goodness. Although he did keep looking at me during the meeting. I could have fainted when I saw him and realized who he was. I think if he had mentioned that day I probably would have fainted. I was kind of rude to him."

"Well, I'm sure he's forgotten all about that day by now, so tell me all about it--this is so exciting."

"The benefits are really good. I'll get another week of vacation, because they are grandfathering in our time with Sunrise. The medical is better, and they have vision and dental coverage, which I didn't have before, and, as I said, the raise on top of everything else--this is really a great opportunity."

"Mom, this is just incredible. Things have really started to turn around in the last couple of months. It looks like the new year holds a lot of promise."

CHAPTER 11

When they return to work after the long New Year's weekend, there is another staff meeting. This time Bill is the only one on site, but Ed Clancy and Lisa Morrison, the head of HR. are conferenced in. As everyone settles in, Bill welcomes them.

"Good morning, everyone. I'm very happy that all of you have decided to stay with Sullivan Enterprises. We received everyone's acceptance letters over the weekend and I appreciate you all getting those back to us so quickly. Lisa will be contacting each of you individually to go over the benefits enrollment procedures, so please don't hesitate to contact her at any time if you have questions."

"As you all know from your introductory packets, we will be keeping the name of Sunrise Printing. It's well known and respected in the printing industry. I want to really grow this business, and I know we already have a good customer base, but now with bringing all of Sullivan Enterprises' printing and graphics work on board, we will be on the fast track of expansion.

"I think we have a great leadership team here with Hector and Cate, and I will be working very closely with them for the next few months to help integrate Sunrise with Sullivan, and incorporate the vision I have for Sunrise. We'll be making a couple of title changes to follow Sullivan's naming conventions, and that will all be communicated to you by email later this week. I'll be taking Mr. Lawden's old office while I'm here, and I believe in an open-door policy, so if you have any questions, or concerns, please feel free to come in and speak with me.

"I know you all have a lot of projects in the works, and we don't want to start off our new adventure by missing due dates, so as promised, I will keep this brief. Hector, Cate--if you could stay behind, I'd like to get with you on a few things."

Once everyone else is out of the room, Bill closes the door so he can dive a little deeper into the changes he wants to make with Hector and Cate. "Hector, you've been in this business a long time, so I'm counting on you to hire some top-notch people as we expand."

"Sure, boss. How soon do you think we will need to start looking?"

"Start right away. I want you to tell me what we're going to need. I'm having my assistant Laura email you all the printing requirements for the past two years for all of Sullivan's businesses. I want you to analyze it along with Sunrise's past two years' business, and let me know what staffing requirements we need to meet the demand."

"Wow, okay. How soon do you want it?" Hector is a little wary of the idea of how much more work this will mean for him.

Bill can see that Hector's used to things rolling along as usual and hopes he will be able to adjust to the faster pace of big business as he replies, "I'd like it by the end of the week. As I said, this is going to move pretty fast."

Hector being a glass half empty kind of guy, asks, "What about this place? I mean, we have some room to expand here, but depending on the volume, we may need a bigger place."

Bill just smiles and says, "Give me your estimates and we'll see what we're dealing with."

He then turns to Cate. "Now, Cate, your role is going to get a lot bigger."

She isn't sure what that means, but she feels a little wave of excitement pass through her as she thinks, *Well, that really made Hector's eyes widen.*

Bill continues, "I would like for you to hire an assistant to take over some of your work, so you can be more involved in helping me grow this business."

Now, she looks surprised. "An assistant? Okay, but I've never hired anyone before."

"That's okay; Lisa will take care of setting everything up for you, and we can even have her in on the interviews if you like. But I want you to make the final decision. This is someone you will be working very closely with." Lisa chimes in and does a quick rundown of the normal hiring procedures and tries to let Cate know that she's not in this alone.

As Lisa finishes, Bill continues, "I also want you both to understand that with your new positions, you are now on an equal level."

Now Cate doesn't know whose eyes are wider, hers or Hector's. She can see from the look on Hector's face that he doesn't like this at all.

Bill goes on, "Hector, your new title will be Operations Manager, as such, you are responsible for the daily operations--the quality, the pricing, the deadlines, hiring decisions for the print and warehouse personnel. Cate, your new title will be Business Manager, and you will be responsible for the finance and marketing portion of the business staff. And, yes, I think it will grow into a staff. Of course, you will both have to learn our corporate policies and procedures. But I will have a team assigned to bringing you onboard and getting you up to speed quickly. I know this is a lot, but I promise it will be a great ride."

As Cate returns to her office, she has the urge to do her happy dance just thinking about the look on Hector's face. She knows Hector well enough to know that he thinks going from VP to Operations Manager is a definite demotion, at least in his mind. Even though he will probably have more responsibility and she's sure a lot more money, she knows that he will see it differently, but he can't make her life hell anymore.

CHAPTER 12

That evening after Cate has the girls tucked into bed and has time to sit on the couch and relax, she reflects on her day. *Man, he makes my head spin. Those eyes! My God, they are so intense. How can I concentrate when he looks at me like that? I don't know if I'm the right person for what he has in mind. Hiring an assistant and having a staff. This is so out of my league. But I have to make this work; this is such a wonderful opportunity for me professionally and personally. Especially since Mom probably won't be able to go back to work, this is our chance to finally get on track financially. I have to do it.*

Phoebe sees that Cate is in deep thought and asks if everything is alright.

"Yeah, I was just thinking about everything that happened at work today. It's just a little overwhelming. Mr. Sullivan, Bill, has some very big plans for our little printing business, and I just hope I can meet his expectations."

Phoebe smiles and sits next to Cate. "You never give yourself enough credit--you know that business front and back. Honey, Mr. Lawden used to always tell me how happy he was with you. He said he knew you were always looking out for him. Making sure all the billing was done on time and always on top of the collections. All you have to do is be yourself and it will work out fine."

"Mom, I sure hope you're right. Bill did say we would

have a team to help us get on board with this new corporate culture. I guess you're right; I'll just have to take it one day at a time.

"Bill is changing my title from Office Manager to Business Manager and is talking about me having a staff of people one day. I never really thought about managing other people. It's exciting and scary at the same time. The best part is that now Hector is the Operations Manager instead of VP, and Bill explicitly said that Hector and I are now on the same level. You should have seen Hector's face when he heard that."

"Seems like you like your new boss so far, he must be nice if he lets you call him Bill. Tell me about him."

"He does seem nice, and he insists we call him Bill. He's about six feet tall, with black hair and has these really intense blue eyes that look right through you. He's in his mid to late thirties. Really young to be the owner of a huge company.

"There are thirteen other companies that fall under Sullivan Enterprises, it's really impressive. I think he likes to take action and move quickly. Bill really wants to build Sunrise into a major business, but I think most of the growth will come from the other Sullivan companies. He told me about the annual meeting of all the Business Managers at the corporate office in Charlotte in a couple of months, and he wants me to go."

"Honey, that sounds great. It's all so exciting." Phoebe is thrilled to see Cate finally having something positive happening for her.

Cate nods her head. "It really is. I think getting together with the other Business Managers will really help me get a grasp on what's expected of me. I was thinking when I get the dates, I'll call Debbie to see if the girls and I can stay there for the week. I'm sure they'll love having them for a whole week."

Cate reins herself in, remembering her mom's condition. "I know it's still a ways off, but I want to make sure you'll be okay here by yourself."

"I'll be fine--besides, it's a couple of months away, and your Aunt Alison either drops by or calls me every day. Between her and Marie next door checking on me all the time, everything will work out. Does it seem like Bill remembers you from the rainstorm?"

With relief visible on her pretty face, she answers, "No, I don't think he does. I would have been so embarrassed. He says he'll be working with us for the next few months to help integrate everything. He's set up in Mr. Lawden's office, so I guess we'll get to know him pretty well."

Saying a silent prayer of thanks, Phoebe takes Cate's hand and kisses her on the cheek. "Honey, I'm so happy for you. It's about time you get a break, so you can get your life back on track and work on a future for you and the girls."

"For all of us. Mom. We're all in this together."

CHAPTER 13

Over the next few weeks, Cate and Bill get to know each other professionally, and they do work very closely--he makes sure of it.

As he promised, there is an integration team of four people assigned to Sunrise to teach Cate and Hector the ins and outs of their business operating system, which was custom-designed by Bill's flagship company, Sullivan Technologies.

There is at least one person on site at all times, but most of the training is done remotely through conference calls and webinars, and Bill sits in on all of them, making sure to always position himself as close to Cate as professionally acceptable.

Bill has daily meetings with Cate and Hector to discuss the progress of all open jobs to ensure they are meeting all deadlines, and to discuss any concerns they may have. He also meets with them individually before the end of the day to discuss how they feel things are progressing within their own responsibilities.

He especially looks forward to the one-on-one time with Cate. He loves breathing in the soft, fresh scent of her perfume. He has to constantly keep himself in check. When they're alone and he's so close to her, he just wants to reach out and brush his hand down her cheek and lean in and kiss that beautiful mouth.

Cate's head has been spinning non-stop. She hasn't felt this challenged and excited in years. She is also very much aware of Bill's presence. He's so handsome, and intense, sometimes it's hard to concentrate when he's so close. She seems to get a little jolt of electricity that runs throughout her body every time he walks in the room. She keeps telling herself it's just nerves because she wants so badly to prove she's capable of this new position he's given her.

She also admires the fact that Bill is not the typical CEO. He's very hands-on and he's made sure to get to know each of his new employees personally by taking some time to sit with each one and learn a little about the daily tasks they perform. He also eats lunch in the lunchroom with everyone a few times a week.

This is something he does during the transition period of every acquisition. Even though his corporation has grown at breakneck speed over the last several years, he still wants to maintain a sense of the small-business, personal touch he grew up admiring in his parents' hardware store. He wants his employees to know he's approachable if they ever have problems or concerns.

Cate goes home every evening exhausted, but elated with how much she's learning and accomplishing. Time has been flying by and she can hardly believe that she leaves tomorrow for the Business Managers' meeting at the corporate office in Charlotte. She can't wait to see the offices and meet the people she's been working with remotely.

CHAPTER 14

As the week long meeting starts to wind down, Cate can't help but think that the last eight weeks have been the best of her professional life. Her job has been more challenging than at any time in the last six plus-years that she's been with Sunrise. She hired an assistant, whom she really likes, and she feels like she has really been proving to Bill that she is a valuable employee and deserving of the trust he has placed in her. She didn't realize how complacent she had become in her job--of course, she knows that she never could have handled this challenge a couple of years ago.

Bill is also reflecting on the last eight weeks as he thinks how hard it's been working so closely with Cate and having to maintain his professional demeanor when all he really wants to do is touch her. As he sits at the desk he hasn't occupied for two months, he goes over his calendar for the next week. Laura walks in and places his mail on the desk and asks if everything is okay, because he's been looking at the same screen for the last fifteen minutes that she's been in and out of his office.

Bill glances at the stack of mail and says, "Laura, thanks for your help arranging all the lunches and dinners for the conference. I don't know how you do it. Please don't ever think about retiring. I couldn't make it without you."

She laughs. “Don’t be silly; I can’t leave you. Who would keep you in line? By the way, it’s good to finally meet the reason for your sudden interest in the printing business.”

Surprised by her comment, he raises his eyebrows, “What do you mean? This was a good business decision. This business has already proven to be beneficial to all of SE.”

“Well, I didn’t say it was a bad decision; all I said was I now understand what got you interested.”

He just shakes his head and chuckles. “Laura, you know me too well. What do you think of her?”

“Well, she’s certainly very pretty--and smart, too. I like her.”

“Do you think I stand a chance?”

“Do I think *YOU* stand a chance? Are you crazy? What woman wouldn’t be attracted to you? Hell, the whole office practically melts when you walk through.”

“Oh, Laura, you just say that because you love me.”

“That is true, I do love you; and yes, I think you stand a chance. I noticed the way she looked at you when she thought no one was watching, but then again, all the women in the room were looking at you that way.”

He leans forward and lowers his voice. “Today’s the last day of the conference, and I happened to overhear that she’s not leaving until tomorrow. How can I get her to go to dinner with me without her thinking I’m asking her on a date? I don’t want to scare her away, or make her think I’m the kind of boss that expects something in return for helping someone advance in their career.”

Laura sits in the chair across from Bill and thinks for a minute. “Hmmm, well...how about inviting her to dinner with you, me, and Ed. Then I’ll come up with a last-minute excuse for not being able to go. When you and Ed get to the restaurant, he can get an emergency phone call on some legal dilemma and have to leave."

"That's good. I'm liking it."

"Here's an idea. You can ride with Ed; then she'll have to bring you home."

"Okay, okay. This is good. Are you sure everyone else is leaving today? I don't want it to look like I'm singling her out."

"Yes, I'm sure. Everyone else is leaving between 2 and 3 p.m. to get to the airport."

This brings a big smile to his face. "Okay. Would you call Sal's and let them know I'll need my table for tonight?" Bill walks around the desk and hugs Laura and gives her a kiss on the forehead. "You are a devious genius."

CHAPTER 15

When Cate gets back to her in-laws' that afternoon, she calls Phoebe as she does every day. "Hi, Mom. Just checking in to see how everything is going."

Phoebe has gotten much stronger and is feeling more like her old self every day. "Everything is fine. Alison and I went to the movies today and we're waiting for your Uncle Kirk to get home, so we can go out to dinner. How's everything going there?"

"It's great--this week has been packed with information, and meeting with the other Business Managers has really given me a boost. Everyone has been so nice and helpful. I really learned a lot."

"That's great, honey. How are the girls?"

"Kaylee and Shawn have been enjoying their time with Pat and Debbie. I'm glad they've been able to spend a lot of quality time with the girls. I think they needed it as much as the kids. Of course, they have been spoiling them rotten, but that's okay."

"Yes, it is. They don't get to spend nearly enough time with them."

"We'll be driving back home in the morning. Tonight, I'm going to dinner with Bill, his assistant Laura, and Ed, the head of legal. Everyone else left today, but when he found out I wasn't leaving until tomorrow, he asked me to join them. I thought that was pretty nice."

"He must like you a lot."

"I hope so. I've really been trying hard to prove I'm worthy of all the responsibility he's given me."

"Do you think he likes you a little more than just professionally?"

"What? Oh, Mom, don't be silly."

"What's silly about that? Cate, you're a beautiful, intelligent woman. Men, all men, find that very attractive--and what about you? You're always telling me how handsome he is, and you're always talking about his intense blue eyes. Maybe you like him a little more than professionally too?"

Cate smiles and says, "Well, he is handsome, maybe under different circumstances I might be attracted to him, but I'm not ready to even think about another man yet. Besides, he's my boss, and it's never a good idea to get into a relationship with your boss. So many things can go wrong, and you know how people like to talk. Besides, it's usually the woman that always comes out on the losing end."

Phoebe shrugs. "Well--not always, and as for you not being ready, I think you should start getting out into the social scene again. You're too young to let this be it for you."

"Mom, we're not getting into this conversation now. It's a moot point. I'll see you tomorrow afternoon. I love you--bye."

CHAPTER 16

Cate is right on time as she walks into Sal's Restaurant. Bill and Ed are standing at the hostess' station waiting for the hostess to return. Bill smiles when he sees her walk in. "Glad you could join us. Unfortunately, Laura had a minor emergency with one or her dogs. Seems when she got home, one of them had been stung by a bee, or something and half of his face was swollen, so she's taking him to the vet."

"Oh no! I hope he'll be okay. I'm sorry she can't join us; I really like her."

Just then the hostess reappears and immediately recognizes Bill, as she subconsciously reaches up to smooth her hair and puts on her best smile. "Mr. Sullivan, so nice to see you again. Your table is ready; please follow me."

Cate notices that she doesn't even glance at the reservation book. "You must come here often. They seem to know you pretty well."

"I do. This is my favorite place to bring business associates, and the food is fantastic. I hope you like Italian." He pulls out Cate's chair and turns to the hostess. "Patty, would you have a bottle of wine sent over, please?"

Thrilled that he remembered her name, she smiles even wider. "Right away, Mr. Sullivan."

As they pick up their menus, Bill asks Ed if he already knows what he'll be ordering. Without even looking at the menu, Ed says, "I think I may have the lasagna. It's always my favorite when I come here." Suddenly Ed pulls his phone from his inside coat pocket. "Oh, hold on, let me take this call, excuse me." Ed steps away from the table to take his call just as Patty returns with a bottle of wine in a chilled bucket and opens it at the table, pouring a little into Bill's glass. He swirls it, takes a taste, and nods his approval. He turns his full attention to Cate. "I hope you like wine--they keep a few special bottles here for me."

Cate always gets just a little disarmed when he looks at her so intently, "Yes, I like wine, but I can only have one glass. I'm not much of a drinker, and I have to drive."

He smiles that smile and says, "I understand." Thankfully Ed returns to the table, and Bill turns to him. "Is everything okay?"

Ed looks truly disappointed. "Not really. We have a potential problem with the contract on the Continental Industries job. Looks like I'll have to go back to the office to get this straightened out." Bill places his glass back on the table and asks, "Do I need to be in on this?"

Ed shakes his head. "No, not yet. I'll let you know if we can't get this ironed out. But since you rode with me, you will have to call for a car, unless Ms. Wilson wants to drive you home."

Cate is surprised, but agrees, "Well, yes. I guess I could drive you. Is it very far?"

"No, not at all. I have a place here downtown. Ed, don't worry about me. Call if you need me; if not, we'll talk in the morning."

Cate starts to panic, thinking, *What the hell? It's just him and me? What in the world will we talk about?* As Ed walks away and Cate starts to sweat, Bill suggest they order an appetizer while they decide what they want to eat.

After they place their orders, Bill turns to Cate and smiles that smile again. "I just wanted to let you know that I think you're doing a great job. I know the last few weeks have been pretty hectic, but you and Hector have really stepped up to the plate. I've been watching you, and I'm very impressed. You've caught on to our system and policies very quickly. You make it look easy, and I hope you are enjoying working with us so far?"

Cate is still a little on edge, but feels more comfortable talking about work. "Thank you. I've been trying very hard and everyone has been so helpful when I have questions. This has been a wonderful opportunity, and yes, I'm really enjoying working for Sullivan Enterprises."

Bill wants so much to reach out and touch her hand, so he picks up a piece of bread instead. "Glad to hear it. I'm really glad you decided to have dinner with me—I mean, us. Just me now. I understand you've been staying with relatives for the week. Are you from this area?"

"No. I'm from Charleston; my in-laws live here. Well, about twenty minutes out, in the Davidson area. So, it was convenient to stay with them. I was able to bring my daughters with me and let them spend some time with their grandparents, it worked out really well. My mother had a stroke last year and still has some weakness in her left arm and leg, so she can't watch them alone yet."

"Will your mom be okay?"

"Yes, she's been doing great. She is making remarkable progress. She was chosen for a case study with Dr. Donaldson--he's a very well-known neurologist, and it's made all the difference."

"Is that Ben Donaldson?"

"Yes. Do you know him?"

"He's a good friend of mine. He went to med school with my brother. He beats me at golf all the time. Glad your mom could get in with him; he's the best on the East coast. It sounds like you and your mom are very close."

Amazingly, Cate feels her nerves start to settle down ever so slightly. "We are. She's my best friend."

Sensing that he's found something else that Cate is comfortable talking about besides work, Bill continues on the same topic. "That's great. I'm close with my family, too."

"Family is very important. Do they live in the Charlotte area?"

"My brother does, he's an orthopedic surgeon. Specializing in sports medicine. He, his wife, and my three nephews live here in Charlotte. We're actually from the Charleston area too. My parents and my sister and her family live there. My home is in Charleston, but I keep an apartment here and drive home most weekends, when I'm not traveling. Do you have any siblings?"

"No. I'm an only child. Always wanted a sister, though. You know, someone to share all your childhood secrets with."

"Yeah, that is great." He glances at her glass and notices it's almost empty. "How did you like the wine?"

"Oh, it's great, and so is the food. This is a wonderful place. I'm glad you invited me."

"My pleasure." He flashes that smile again. The conversation remains light as they finish their dinner.

He finally says, "Look, if it's too much trouble for you to take me home, I'll grab a taxi. I don't want to put you out."

Things have really gone well, not tense at all, so Cate says, "No, no, it's fine. I don't mind."

As he finishes signing the bill, he's thinking, *I don't want this evening to end.* "Okay, then, if you're ready, we can head out."

After a little more small talk on the drive, Cate is relieved that his building is less than ten minutes from the restaurant. As she parks at the curb, he thanks her for the ride and adds, "Would you like to come up for a cup of coffee? I've got this new cappuccino machine, and I'm still learning how to use it."

Cate is surprised, and a wave of fear passes over her. "No, I should be getting home. It's getting late."

Flashing that magical smile, he tries to convince her. "Come on, it's only eight o'clock, and it's just a cup of coffee. I haven't had anyone to try it on yet."

Warning bells are going off. She says, "Oh, I don't know," but is thinking, *No, Cate, not a good idea.*

He doesn't want to push, but he doesn't want to let her go just yet. "I promise I'm not trying to lure you up to my apartment to take advantage of you. It's really just coffee."

She pauses for a moment, then says, "Okay, one cup--then, I have to get home to my girls." *What am I saying?*

That gorgeous smile gets even wider. "Deal."

As they enter his apartment, Cate is blown away. "Wow, this is some place. I've never been in a penthouse before. The view is spectacular, just like in the movies."

He enjoys seeing her eyes sparkle as she takes in the view of Charlotte. "Thanks. It's nice, but I'd rather be at my house in Charleston. That's home."

He starts about the business of making the coffee; he doesn't want her to think it was just an excuse to get her up there. They take their coffee onto the terrace, and Bill points out several points of interest. They are both very aware of how close he stands to her as he does his best to impress her with his knowledge of the city.

She can't really hear what he's saying because her pulse is pounding in her ears. As they finish with the coffee, he knows he has to let her go. He can't think of any more excuses without it getting weird, and if he has to breathe her in any longer, he may explode.

"Cate, thanks for having coffee with me. I really enjoyed the company, and the conversation was great. I talk to a lot of people all the time, but have very few real quality conversations. I'll be traveling all next week, but plan on being back at Sunrise the following week. I look forward to seeing you then. Be careful driving back home tomorrow." He wants so much to lean in and kiss her, but instead he turns and walks to the door.

As Cate drives back to Pat and Debbie's, she can't get him off her mind. She admits to herself that "*IF*" she was interested in dating again, he would be a great start. Falling asleep that night, she keeps thinking of his gorgeous eyes and disarming smile. *Knock it off, Cate; he's your boss.*

CHAPTER 17

When Cate arrives home Saturday afternoon, she's glad that the drive is not any longer, because the girls were getting restless and cranky, but she knows there is little chance of them taking a nap. She's also glad to see her mom is already home, hoping she will entertain the girls while Cate unpacks and gets some laundry done.

Phoebe greets them at the door and takes over the girls right away. She really missed them and thinks they've grown in the week they've been gone. Cate kisses Phoebe and mouths a thank you to her as she walks in the door loaded down with their suitcases. She gets right to work unpacking and washing clothes, and doesn't stop until it's time for dinner.

After dinner, when the kitchen is cleaned, and the girls are bathed and settled in playing with their toys on the living room floor, she finally gets a chance to sit. Phoebe makes them each a cup of tea and they sit back on the sofa to relax and talk. "So how was your week? Tell me all about it--what did you learn, and how was your dinner last night?"

Cate looks over her cup and smiles. She knows her mother has been dying to hear the details. "Mom, I learned so much last week. I have a ton of notes to go through, but everyone was great. I got to meet everyone I've been talking to over the last couple of months and put faces with names.

"The other Business Managers were so helpful, and it really made me feel good to know they've all felt just as overwhelmed as I have. I made a lot of great contacts that can help me with system questions and shortcuts, and dinner wound up being just Bill and me. Laura had an emergency with one of her dogs, and Ed got a call shortly after we got to the restaurant and had to leave."

Phoebe's eyes widen, and she sits up a little straighter, "Really? Do tell."

"It was really nice. We talked a little about work; then he asked about who I was staying with there, and he told me a little about his family. He's actually from here in Charleston and most of his family still lives in the area. He said he decided on Charlotte for the corporate headquarters because it's the hub of business in the area, but still close enough to come home on weekends. He's very close with his family; you can tell when he talks about them, and I think he really likes kids. He speaks a lot about his niece and nephews."

"Well, that sounds like some dinner. Did the restaurant have to kick you out at closing?"

"No, actually, I had to drive him home because he rode with Ed. So, when Ed had to leave, he didn't have a ride."

Phoebe's eyes get wide. "Uh-oh!"

Cate glances down into her cup and smiles. "Well, I did go up to his penthouse apartment. But only for a cup of coffee."

Uh-oh!"

"Yes, it was all very proper, but it does seem like he's kind of lonely. I guess that happens when you're a big businessman. Lots of people around you all the time but still alone, that kind of thing."

"Well, it sure seems like you two hit it off pretty good. So, are you still going to tell me you don't think he likes you a little more than professionally?"

"Oh, Mom, don't be silly."

"Cate, do you really think he invites all of his employees up to his apartment for coffee?" Of course, coffee is said with the little air quotes. "And I think you may like him too."

"Oh, don't start that again. I told you, I'm not interested in starting anything up with anyone. I've got enough to deal with without adding a man to my agenda."

Phoebe just smiles and says, "Mmm-hmmm."

CHAPTER 18

Cate arrives to work early Friday morning thinking how quickly this week has gone by. She's been so busy getting caught up from being in Charlotte the week before that she hasn't had much time to think about anything else, but now she starts to realize how much she missed having Bill in the office this week. As she sits drinking her cup of coffee, going through her email, it dawns on her how anxious she is to see Bill again. She reflects on their dinner, especially the coffee at his place afterward. She smiles and thinks, *"IF" I were interested in trying the dating pool again, which I definitely am not, I wouldn't mind testing the waters with him.*

Catching herself, she shakes her head. *Oh, stop, Cate-- don't be silly. A man like that probably has women falling all over him. He can have anyone he wants; why on earth would he be interested in someone like me? Get your head out of the clouds and keep it strictly business. I don't need my heart broken again, and I will never have what I had with Sean, so I need to get my head straight.* Just then her phone rings and brings her back to reality. When she answers, she's stunned to hear Bill on the other end.

"Hi, Cate. It's Bill. How's everything going?"

It takes her a moment to adjust. *Did he hear me thinking about him? He must be psychic.* "Everything's going great. We got the Tri-Star job out two days early, and Hector says it looks like the Sea Breeze Boating order will be done right on schedule." She tries to shake off the little twinge of excitement she felt when she heard his voice.

Bill has been thinking about their dinner all week too and decides he's tired of waiting, and being the man of action that he is, he gets right to the point.

"That's great--you and Hector are doing a great job. Listen, I fly back into Charleston this evening, and I was wondering if you would have dinner with me tomorrow night?"

Cate is a little taken aback. "I, um, on Saturday? I guess if it's really important."

She can hear the little laugh in his voice as he says, "It's a date, Cate. I'm asking you on a date."

Now she is totally floored. "OH! Well... I. I'm not sure that's such a good idea. I mean, working together and you being my boss. I don't know."

Again, he cuts right to the chase. "Great. I'll pick you up at 7, and it's casual, so I'll see you tomorrow. My plane's boarding now, gotta go."

She sits there holding the humming phone to her ear. *What!? A DATE!? I'm not ready to date.*

CHAPTER 19

By Saturday evening, Cate has worked herself into a tizzy. She's so nervous she hasn't been able to eat a thing all day. She turns to Phoebe for the hundredth time. "Mom, what am I doing? I can't do this. I can't go on a date. I have two children and a job that takes up all my time. I'm not ready to date. I'm calling him to cancel. I'll say I'm sick and can't make it."

Phoebe takes Cate by the hand and leads her to the kitchen table. As they sit she smiles, thinking Cate is so cute. "Cate, stop. You're not calling and cancelling. This is exactly what you need. Having a nice dinner with a nice man is not going to stop you from taking care of your children, or your job."

"But Mom, he's my boss."

"Honey, he asked you out because he's attracted to you. He didn't pressure you, or make you feel like you had to date him to keep your job, did he?"

"No, but...."

"No buts. Look, this is more dangerous for him than it is for you. He's willing to put himself in a precarious position by asking an employee out. I mean, with the way people like to sue over everything these days."

"Oh, I would never do that. He's not like that. We had a really nice dinner in Charlotte and he was a perfect gentleman."

"See, nothing to worry about, and I'll give him the once-over when he gets here. You know I have a good sense of judgment about people."

"But Mom, what will people think?"

"People will think it's about time you start living again."

"But what about Sean?"

"Oh, honey, Sean loved you very much, and he would want you to find happiness again. Maybe it is, and maybe it's not with this guy, but you've got to open yourself up again."

"I just don't want to feel the pain I felt when I lost Sean."

"I know--but look, this is only one dinner. If you don't want to see him again, you just let him know it's still too soon. He should be able to understand that, but give yourself a chance to have a little fun."

Cate sits up straight and grabs her chest. "Oh my God--I just heard a car door. I think that's him."

Phoebe pats her hand and gets up. "Calm down. Go give the girls kisses, and I'll get the door."

When Phoebe opens the door, she's surprised at how good-looking Mr. Sullivan is.

Bill flashes that charming smile and extends his hand. "Hi, Mrs. Carter. I'm Bill Sullivan."

Phoebe takes his hand in both of hers and leads him into the living room. "Hi, Bill, come on in--and call me Phoebe. Cate is just saying good-bye to the girls."

As he waits for Cate, he notices a picture on the mantel of Cate with a handsome young man and a baby. He looks at the family photo and silently hopes she's ready to give him a chance. Phoebe makes small talk, as she tries to gauge her first impression of him.

After a few minutes Cate enters the room dressed in black jeans and a jade-green satiny blouse that brings out her eyes. "Hi, sorry to keep you waiting."

The first thing he notices is how great she looks in jeans; he's used to seeing her in dresses, or slacks. Then he sees how nervous she looks. "No worries--your mom and I have been getting to know one another."

Cate turns to Phoebe, and for a moment wants to say, *Please don't make me go*, but instead says, "Mom, I think the girls are pretty much settled for the night. They're watching *Frozen*, again, and Beth will be over in a little while to help you. I won't be too late." She gives her mom a kiss on the cheek. "Love you."

As they get into his car, she can barely breathe. She doesn't know what to say, she feels so awkward.

Bill wonders if he pushed too soon. "Why do you look so nervous?"

She decides honesty is the best policy. "Because I am. Honestly, I almost called you to cancel, but my mom wouldn't let me."

"Well, I'll have to thank your mom, but Cate, I don't want to make you nervous. I just enjoyed your company so much last week. I thought about our dinner and the way conversation with you was just so easy and relaxed. I'm sorry if I came on too strong, but I just wanted to see you again." The look in his eyes says he's genuinely concerned.

"No, it's okay. This is the first time I've been out with anyone other than my mom and my daughters since my husband's death. Honestly, I don't know if I'm ready for this."

He tries to understand how she must be feeling. "Look, I promise no pressure. It's just dinner. Just give it a try and if you decide you don't want to go out with me again, I'll back off and be Mr. Professional again, okay?"

She's a little relieved to hear that he will understand if she isn't ready, so she lets out her breath, which she didn't even realize she had been holding. "Okay, thanks, I appreciate that. So, where are we going?"

"Well, I had this crazy idea that maybe we could go back to my house and I could grill a couple of steaks and we could just talk and get to know one another."

She feels the blood drain from her face. "To your house?"

He sees it too. "Too much? If that's a bad idea, we can go out for steaks."

"Honestly, this all makes me very nervous."

"I know, but if you just give me a chance, I promise you'll enjoy the evening, and as soon as you're ready to leave, we will. It's your call."

She's not sure what to do. She finally says, "Okay, I guess since I've already been to your apartment, I might as well see your house too."

This brings a smile back to his face. "Great. I really grill a mean steak."

As they drive, he tells her about his week and asks her about hers. He knows talking about work is her comfort zone and wants to help her to relax a little.

About thirty minutes later, they drive through beautiful iron gates, up a long winding driveway through a grove of oak trees that opens up to a beautiful manicured lawn. They pull into a circular brick driveway in front of the biggest house Cate has ever seen.

Bill gets out and rushes around to open Cate's door. He waves his hand toward the house. "Well, this is it."

She's amazed at how beautiful everything is as they approach the door. Cate is looking around like a kid in a candy store. "Wow, this is incredible."

They enter through the leaded glass doors and as she moves through the foyer, all Cate can think is, *What the hell am I doing here? I don't belong in this world.* Bill takes her hand and leads her toward the kitchen. "Come on in--I'm going to need some help in here. You any good at salads?"

She feels like she's in a dream. "Salads? Sure, I can manage that."

They enter a huge open sparkling kitchen and Bill points to the refrigerator. "Okay, everything you need is right there in the fridge; make yourself at home. I'm going outside to get the grill ready."

Cate stands there looking at the huge Sub-Zero refrigerator thinking, *Wow, I knew it would be a big house, but I wasn't expecting a mansion. This kitchen is bigger than half of our house.* She opens the refrigerator door and says to herself, *Well, he was right-- everything I need is here. Looks like he bought out the store.*

Bill comes up behind her and startles her a little when he says, "I got a couple of filets. How do you like yours?"

"Oh, umm, medium well." She reaches in the fridge and starts pulling out all the salad fixings and tries to play it cool. "Is there anything you don't like in your salad?"

"Nope. I eat just about anything, so fix them the way you like. Would you like a glass of wine while we get this going?"

"Sure, that sounds good."

As she fixes the salads and sips her wine she thinks, *Maybe Mom's right; I should relax and just enjoy an evening out. I think my last adult evening out was before Sean left us. Wow, this wine is really good.*

Bill's been going in and out of the kitchen to the patio, but now he finally has everything cooking and comes over to refill their glasses. "How's the salad coming?"

"Done. Which dressing do you like?"

"I have a great balsamic in the fridge. I'll take that."

"Sounds good. I'll try that too."

He starts picking up the salad bowls. "Let's bring everything outside. I thought we could eat on the patio since it's such a beautiful night, and I started a fire."

Cate gets the silverware and follows him outside. "Oh, this is really nice. I love your patio."

He pulls her chair out and sets her salad in front of her. "Thanks. I spend most of my time out here. This grill gets a lot more work than the stove. I grill just about everything."

He sits across the table from her and takes a forkful of salad. "Hmm, very good. Steaks should be done in a few minutes."

By the time they finish their salad, a little timer goes off signaling the steaks are done. He dishes them out with a side of asparagus wrapped in bacon. As he sits back down, he looks directly into her eyes. "I'm glad you agreed to have dinner here with me. Eating out is great, but you can't get this atmosphere at any restaurant."

There's that twinge of excitement in her stomach again as she smiles in agreement. "I'm glad, too. This is really nice and relaxing."

Bill lifts his wine glass. "Let's raise our glasses to good food, good atmosphere, and great conversation."

CHAPTER 20

When they finish their meal, they move to the chairs closer to the fire. Bill pulls a blanket out of a side table and says, "It's good to see you so relaxed."

Wrapping the blanket around her shoulders, she agrees, "I think it must be the wine and the fire--and of course a full stomach always helps, too."

He sits back admiring how beautiful she is, happy that he can study her without worrying about anyone seeing. "You know, the only people I usually feel comfortable with are my family, but with you it's just so easy. I'm talking to people all the time between business meetings, staff meetings, and lunches, but it's good to just sit and talk to someone I really want to talk to."

Now she looks directly into his eyes. "Why?"

"Why, what?"

"Why do you really want to talk to me?"

Meeting her eyes, he answers, "Since the first day I saw you, you intrigued me. You're beautiful, Cate. What man wouldn't want to talk to you? You've got that beautiful, thick, long auburn hair and those amazing big green eyes. That first day, you knocked me off my feet."

She wasn't ready for this much honesty. "Oh, I...."

He takes her hand. "Don't be embarrassed--you are beautiful. Since that very first day I've wanted to kiss you, and working so close to you these last few months has only made that worse. But, I won't until you tell me you're ready. The last thing I want to do is scare you away."

She pulls her eyes from his and glances down at her hands, the way she does whenever she's nervous. "Bill, I'm very confused right now. I'm very attracted to you, but I don't know if I'm ready to start dating again. I haven't dated since high school."

"Were you and your husband high school sweethearts?"

"No, I met Sean my freshman year in college. We had one of those awful group projects together with two other people. We would meet at a coffee shop near campus, and he and I would stay afterward and talk for hours. I don't know, it was just an immediate attraction.

"Sean decided after freshman year that college wasn't for him. He had always wanted to join the Marines, so he did. We got married right after I graduated. We had Kaylee a year later then I got pregnant with Shawn."

"He was on his last deployment, two months short of getting out when his convoy ran over an IED and all six men in his Humvee were killed. I was six months pregnant with a two-year-old and suddenly, I was a widow and a single mom. I couldn't have made it if it wasn't for my mother. I don't even remember much from the time I got the news until Shawn was born. Those three months are all a blur. We hadn't even picked out a name yet, so I decided to name her after her father, just spelled differently.

"When I held Shawn for the first time, I finally snapped out of the fog I'd been in and realized that I was all these two little girls had. I had to find a way to support them and love them and raise them alone."

She's suddenly embarrassed. "I'm sorry. I don't usually just pour all of this out on people. In fact, this is actually the first time I've really talked about all of this to anyone but my mom."

He kisses her hand that he's been holding. "Don't be sorry. I'm glad you feel comfortable enough with me to open up."

"It's strange, but for some reason, I do feel comfortable talking to you. What about you? Have you ever been married, any kids?"

He answers with a little laugh, "No. I've never met anyone before that I really felt enough of a connection with to get serious. In fact, the last girl I was serious about was Alicia Stone. We were high school seniors. We dated all through senior year, then we went to different colleges and she met someone else. Broke my heart."

"Seems like we both opened up a bit."

"Yes, I guess we did."

Cate notices the clock on the kitchen wall. "Oh my, it's really getting late and I should get home. Let me help you get this all cleaned up."

As she starts to get up, he grabs her hand again. "Cate, I want to see you again."

"I'd like that too, but I don't know if it's a good idea. I really don't want anyone at work to know that I'm seeing the boss."

"I understand. I've been hanging out at Sunrise much longer than I have at any of the other acquisitions. I'll go back to my Charlotte office if you will promise to see me on weekends."

She starts to feel the butterflies waking up again. "I don't want to get ahead of ourselves. Can we just take this one day at a time?"

"Absolutely. I won't push too hard. I'll let you set the pace."

"Thanks."

CHAPTER 21

When Phoebe gets up the next morning, Cate is already in the kitchen with a cup of coffee, and starting to mix pancake batter for when the girls wake up. Cate hands her a cup of coffee as she sits at the table. She's surprised to see Cate up so early, since she knows she got in late.

"Good morning. I didn't hear you come in last night. How was the date? Where did you go?"

"It went well. Actually, we went to his house, he grilled steaks, and we ate on his patio by the fire. It was really nice."

Phoebe raises her eyebrows. "His house? Hmmm."

"Oh, Mom. He was again the perfect gentleman. I was so nervous at first, but once we sat down to eat and started talking, it was really good. He's very easy to talk to. It's crazy, but I feel comfortable with him. Maybe it's because we've been working so closely the last few months, I don't know... but I like him. But it still seems too soon to think of being with someone else. What will people think?"

"What people? Cate, anyone who knew you and Sean knows how much you loved one another, and they know how devastated you were at his death, and how hard things have been for you since. And people that didn't know the two of you really don't matter."

"But what about everyone at work? I can't have them thinking I'm getting preferential treatment, or that I'm trying to advance in the company by dating the boss. And what about Pat and Debbie? I'm sure Sean's parents aren't going to be too happy to see me dating someone else."

"Cate, Pat and Debbie love you like a daughter, and as long as this man is good to you and the girls, I think they will accept it. As for the people at work, you've worked with most of them for a long time now and they know how hard you work. Honey, people will think what they think; you can't control that."

Cate sits down at the table next to Phoebe and puts her head in her hands. "I know, but it would really bother me to know they thought that way about me, and I don't want to do anything to hurt Pat and Debbie."

Taking one of Cate's hands away from her head and squeezing it, Phoebe smiles. "Honey, you, finding happiness again shouldn't hurt them. Sure, it will seem strange to see you with someone else, but they know you're too young to just stop living. You vowed to love, honor, and cherish Sean until death do you part, and you honored those vows. But now it's time for you to join the land of the living again."

"Unfortunately, Kaylee and Shawn will never know how truly great Sean was. All they will ever have of him are pictures and stories. The three of you need someone to love you and hold you, and the girls will need a father to teach them how a man should treat a woman. Now, it may not be this guy, but you've got to allow it to develop in order to find out."

Cate gets up and hugs her mom. "How do you always know the right things to say?"

"I'm a mom--we know everything."

A small, shy grin lifts the edges of Cate mouth. "He said he wants to see me again...soon. Maybe I'll invite him over here for dinner, so you can get to know him, and he can see that with me comes a whole family. I'd like to gauge his reaction to this reality early on."

Nodding, Phoebe agrees. "Good idea. You let me know when, and I'll make my famous spaghetti."

CHAPTER 22

Monday morning, Cate is in her office sorting through what has to be billed when her phone rings. She picks it up on the second ring. "Good morning, Cate Wilson."

The voice on the other end stops her in her tracks. "Well, good Monday morning, Cate Wilson. I just wanted to say thanks for having dinner with me Saturday evening. I really enjoyed it. I wanted to call you yesterday but didn't know if that would be too soon. I couldn't wait any longer--sorry."

She smiles as she feels that little twinge in her stomach. "Don't be sorry. I wanted to talk to you too."

A sense of relief washes over Bill. He had been debating for an hour whether he should call her this morning, or not. "Good--I'm glad you're thinking about me; that gives me hope. I just wanted to let you know I'll be stopping by the office this morning to clear out my things before heading to Charlotte. Do you think we could have lunch before I leave?"

The butterflies fly into a tizzy in her stomach. "I would like to, but I don't think that's a good idea. I don't want people starting to talk already."

She can hear the disappointment in his voice when he says, "Okay, but can I see you this weekend then?"

"Yes, I'd like that very much. I was thinking maybe you could come to my house this time. I'd like you to see what an evening in my life is like. It's a whole different world from yours."

Now he sounds cheerful again. "That's a great idea. I'd love that. I want to know everything about you, and if you think being around a couple of little girls is going to scare me off, you're wrong."

"We'll see. You know visiting and playing with your niece and nephews is a lot different from living with and being responsible for children all the time."

"I know. I told you, I'm very close with my family and I see what my sister and brother go through with their kids. I know it's not all fun and games. So, can we make it Saturday evening? I'll probably get in late Friday."

"That sounds good. Does 6:30 work for you? The girls eat early, their bed time is 9:00 on weekends. Oh, I hope you like spaghetti."

"Perfect. I love spaghetti."

Cate smiles as she hangs up the phone, then the devil of doubt enters in as she thinks, *Be careful, Cate; he has no clue what raising children is like. We'll see how long he sticks around once he gets a little taste of what your life is like.*

They're both very busy all week and don't have much chance to talk, but Bill does find time to instant message her at least once a day with just a little hello, or a smiley face. Cate keeps her replies brief, too. She likes that he's thinking about her, but it scares her that she's starting to look forward to these little messages.

By Saturday morning, Cate is exhausted from going back and forth with herself all week on whether she should even let this thing with Bill go any further. She's able to come up with a dozen reasons why this is not a good idea, but only one why she should see where this goes--she likes him. Of course, her mom is all for giving this a chance, but she still has so many doubts.

As she sets about her usual Saturday routine of cleaning and laundry, she catches herself putting a little extra effort into the cleaning. Despite her doubts, she does want to make a good impression.

Once she gets the house straight, she goes to the grocery with Phoebe's list for dinner. Thankfully, she can leave the girls with her mom and Beth while she goes to the store. It sure makes shopping easier, and the girls are having so much fun playing outside in their sandbox.

The day is flying by, and by the time she gets home, her nerves are starting to set in. She helps Phoebe prep everything, then goes to take her shower so she can get the girls ready before Bill arrives.

At 6:00, the doorbell rings. Phoebe opens the door to see Bill Sullivan standing there with a bouquet of flowers and a bottle of wine in his hands. He immediately says, "I know I'm a little early, but thought maybe you ladies could use some help with something." Even as he says it he thinks, *That was pretty lame. Should have just told the truth--you've been dying to get over here all day.*

Phoebe knows the truth, so she just smiles. "Hi, Bill. Good to see you again."

"Good to see you, too Mrs. Carter. I brought flowers for the cook and some wine--I hope you like it."

"Please, call me Phoebe. I shouldn't drink, but I may have to have a little taste. Cate will be right out, she's getting the girls washed for dinner. They were playing in their sandbox and definitely need a little cleaning up. Besides, this will give us a few minutes to talk."

Now it's Bill's turn to get a little nervous. He hasn't been questioned by anyone's parents since high school. "Sure, I'd like that."

As Phoebe leads him into the kitchen so she can get a vase for the flowers and put the wine to chill, she looks him in the eyes and says, "I'll be straight with you--are you looking for this thing between you and Cate to go somewhere, or is this just a conquest for you?"

He's a little shocked. She's direct, but he likes that. "Mrs. Carter—Phoebe--I'm very attracted to your daughter. I know she's been through a hard time, but I'm hoping she'll give me the chance to make her happy again. Honestly, I think there's a better chance of her breaking my heart than the other way around. I was knocked off my feet the first time I saw her, and that's never happened to me before."

Before he can go any further, Cate walks in with both girls in tow and looks from her mom to Bill, knowing they must have been talking about her. "Hi, sorry it took so long. I had to bathe these little beauties. They were two little sand monsters."

Bill's happy to see her and notices again how much her two girls look like her. "No problem. Phoebe and I have just been getting to know one another. So, these are the two young ladies I've heard so much about."

"Yes, this is Kaylee and Shawn. Girls, this is Mr. Bill. He's going to have dinner with us tonight."

Kaylee, never the shy one, immediately goes up to Bill and looking up at him with big green eyes that match her mother's and sister's, she takes his hand. "Hi, Mr. Bill. Do you want to sit next to me?"

"Sure, Kaylee, I'd like that very much. So, is spaghetti your favorite meal?"

"Yes, and Grandma makes the best. It's Shawn's favorite too, but she usually makes a mess."

Dinner conversation is mostly led by Kaylee telling Bill all about her favorite toys, movies, and books in between bites of spaghetti. As they finish, Cate is surprised that she didn't have to remind either of the girls to stop playing and eat. "Well, you girls must have been really hungry today--you both ate all of your dinner without a fuss. Maybe we should let you play in the sandbox every day."

When Cate is wiping off their hands and faces Kaylee asks, "Mom, can Mr. Bill watch a movie with me?"

Cate glances at Bill and laughs. "I don't think Mr. Bill really wants to watch *The Little Mermaid*."

But Bill really does like kids and has enjoyed being entertained by Kaylee throughout dinner, so he jumps in. "What? *The Little Mermaid*? I love Flounder. I'd love to watch some of it with you."

Cate is surprised, but figures he's trying to make a good impression. "You really don't know what you're getting into. Kaylee will narrate the entire movie for you."

Bill, being the businessman, he is, says, "How about we make a deal? I'll watch the first thirty minutes of the movie with you, and then I get to spend some time talking to your mom."

Kaylee thinks for a minute, then agrees, "Okay." Turning to Cate she asks, "Mom, what part is thirty minutes?"

Laughing, Cate answers, "I'm not sure, but I'll let you know. You can watch the first thirty minutes in the living room while Grandma and I clean the kitchen. Then you can finish it in your bedroom." She glances at Bill one more time. "Are you sure you don't mind?"

Kaylee pulls him along into the living room as he replies, "Positive. Ariel is hot."

Thirty minutes later, Cate calls time and Phoebe takes the girls to their room to finish watching the movie allowing Cate and Bill a little time alone. Cate brings in two glasses of wine and sits next to him on the couch. "I think you were a hit with the girls. You really didn't have to watch *Little Mermaid*, though."

He smiles that charming smile. "I didn't mind at all. I love kids, and Kaylee is quite the talker. She's very entertaining."

"Yes, she's not shy. Shawn's a little more reserved, but once she gets to know you, she really opens up too."

He watches her as she sips her wine. "You may think I'm crazy, but I really enjoyed this evening."

"Really?" Cate's not sure if he's sincere, or if he's just saying what she wants to hear.

He sees the doubt in her eyes. "Yes, honestly. I told you I'm very family-oriented. People think I'm some big playboy because I've never been married, but like I told you, that's only because I've never met the right person... until now."

This causes her eyebrows to shoot up. "Oh, so you think I'm the right person?"

He takes her free hand. "Yes, I do. I was attracted to you the first time I saw you--I knew you were someone special. I've never had that happen before. Sure, I've seen beautiful women and thought, 'I want to ask her out,' but when I saw you, it was much more than that."

Not sure what to say, she takes another sip of her wine, and before she can think of a response, Bill asks, "Would it be too much to ask if I could take you and the girls to the zoo tomorrow? I haven't been there in years--the weather is great, and we can have a picnic after."

He continues to surprise her. "Are you sure you want to do that? Believe me, these two can be a handful."

Bill leans over, takes her wine glass and sets it on the coffee table. He holds both her hands and looks deep into her eyes. "I'm sure. Cate, you're not getting it. I really want to be a part of your life, and you have these two amazing little girls--I want to be a part of all of it, if you'll let me."

Still holding on to her skepticism, Cate takes a deep breath. "Bill, you're a good man, but it's just hard for me to understand why you would want to take on a ready-made family when you could have any woman you wanted and start your own family."

He shakes his head. "You *are* the woman I want, and as for the ready-made family, these girls are a part of you and I couldn't be happier about having the chance to spend as much time as I can with the three of you. So, zoo and picnic tomorrow?"

She pauses for a moment, then gives in. "Okay, you're very convincing."

He gives her that killer smile. "Good. I'll pick you up at 10 a.m. and as much as I hate it, I guess I should go, but thanks for the great evening--I really did enjoy it." He pauses at the door and looks deep into her eyes. He brushes her cheek with his fingers and asks softly, "Do you think it would it be okay if I kissed you good night?"

Her stomach jumps at his touch, and a little electric shock passes through her whole body. She's terrified, but manages to whisper, "I think that would be okay." As he leans in she keeps telling herself, *Okay, don't pass out.* With his hand on her cheek, he kisses her soft and slow. Cate feels her knees getting week and steadies herself against the door frame thinking, *Holy crap! I could melt into him so easily.*

He slowly pulls away and just looks at her. "Wow! If I don't leave now, we may be in trouble." It takes all his will power to stop as he keeps reminding himself, *Don't push; you'll scare her away.* He takes a step back. "See you in the morning."

As she watches him walk to his car, she can't move because she's afraid she'll fall. All she can think is, *My God, what am I doing?*

CHAPTER 23

Cate doesn't get much sleep Saturday night. Every time she closes her eyes, she feels his kiss again. She finally gets up at 6:00, and as she's making coffee, Phoebe walks in the kitchen and Cate's glad she's up early too.

Cate pours them each a cup of coffee and sits next to Phoebe at the table. As she absently stirs the cream into her cup she asks, "Mom, what do you think about Bill? He says all the right things, but is it real, or does he just know what to say to get what he wants? I mean, he negotiates for a living."

As Phoebe takes her cup of coffee, she thinks for a minute before answering. "Well, I got a good feeling about him. He seems to be pretty genuine, but only time will tell."

"I'm scared, Mom. What if I fall for him? I mean, it's not just me anymore. What if the girls get attached to him, and then things don't work out...then they get hurt, too?"

Taking a deep breath, Phoebe studies her daughter's face. "Baby, there are no guarantees on anything in life. If you don't take a chance, you don't get hurt, but you could also be missing out on the best things in life."

"Do you think I'm doing the right thing by letting the girls spend time with him already?"

"I think so. He needs to see what family life would be like, and the girls are so young that if he, or you decide it's not working, they will be able to move on easily. We'll just pray about it and leave it in God's hands. He hasn't let us down yet."

Cate hugs her mom. "I don't know what I would do without you. You always help me put things into perspective."

"That's what moms do."

Cate kisses her mom's cheek. "I hope I can guide my daughters as well as you guide me."

Phoebe laughs. "You will; you've had a great teacher. Now you start breakfast and I'll wake the girls so they can eat before you go."

By ten o'clock when Bill arrives, Cate already has the girls and all their stuff ready to go. He's surprised by how much stuff two little bitty girls need. They load the car seats and diaper bag stuffed with diapers, extra clothes, little baggies of snacks, and sippy cups into Bill's SUV. It looks like enough to last for days, and he wonders how long Cate thinks they'll be gone.

After a couple of hours at the zoo, the girls are getting a little bored with it, so they pick up some lunch and take it to the park to eat under the trees. Kaylee and Shawn seem to get a second wind once they're fed and see the swings waiting for them. The girls run toward the swings, and as Cate and Bill walk along behind them, he takes her hand in his thinking, *This is how it's supposed to be. I want this to go on forever.*

Driving home, Bill tries to think of some excuse to keep them longer, or to stay once they get home, but he's not sure she's ready for so much together time. He reaches over and runs his finger across the top of Cate's hand, which sends tiny jolts of electricity all the way up her arm. "Cate, I really enjoyed our day."

She has to struggle to pull her eyes away from watching his finger electrocute her. "Me too. Kaylee and Shawn had a blast." She glances in the back seat. "I'm going to have to wake them up to feed them supper and bathe them."

A little unsure, he asks, "That's good, right?

"Yes, that's good. I think they like you, too."

"Too? So, I guess that means you like me?"

"Yes, I like you."

"Good, that's a start."

As they pull up in front of her house, Cate suddenly gets serious. "Bill, I'm not sure where you see this going, but I don't want my girls to get too attached to you then you lose interest and are gone. I know there are no guarantees in any relationship, but they've been through enough already in their short lives. Please really think this through before they start seeing you as part of their lives."

He grips her hand a little tighter. "I've been thinking this through for some time now, and I have no intention of just coming and going in their lives, or yours. Unless you decide it's not what you want. Believe me, my mom and sister have already let me know that when kids are involved in a relationship you take it slow until you're sure it's what you want, and the more time I spend with you and your daughters, the surer I am. I know you probably think about the fact that I've never committed to anyone, but it's not because I didn't want to be in a relationship. I told you, I've just never met the right person until now."

Looking at him in utter surprise, she's stuck on the words MOM and SISTER. "Wait. You've talked about me to your mom?"

"Of course. Oh, by the way, we're having a little family get- together in a couple of weeks for my dad's birthday. Just a Sunday evening family dinner at my parents' house. Mom wants me to bring you. They're all dying to meet you."

She didn't think it could get worse. "Family dinner? Oh, I don't know. Your whole family will be there--I mean, I don't know."

He gives her hand another little squeeze. "Come on, I met your family."

Cate's finding it a little hard to breathe again. "Yeah, but it's just my mom. You have a whole family. I mean, what will they think? I mean, you're dating an employee."

"Cate, I'm dating a beautiful, kind, thoughtful woman, who happens to work at one of my companies. My family's not a bunch of rich snobs that look down on people. My parents owned a neighborhood hardware store until about fifteen years ago when they retired. They will love you, and while we're making plans, I'd like you to come with me to this fancy-pants awards banquet in Charlotte next month."

Now she's ready to jump out of the car and her mind is going in a dozen directions at once. "What? Oh, I don't know if I'm ready for all of this. I've never been to anything like that. I don't have anything to wear to some fancy dinner. Will people from the office be there?"

"Maybe a couple of them."

"What about keeping this away from work?"

He finally realizes that she's really in a panic. "Calm down. It's a month away, and you know we can't keep this a secret forever, but I'll check to see who's going. Besides, the people I'm closest to at work already know."

She grabs her head. "Oh Lord!"

He can't help thinking how cute she is, but tries to ease her panic with humor. "It's okay, Cate--you're not going to get fired. I know the boss."

She is not amused. "Funny. I'm just concerned about what they'll think. I don't want it to look like I'm getting preferential treatment because I'm dating the boss. I'm not, am I?"

"No, you're not. You work very hard and have earned everything you have. I'm sorry, I didn't mean to get you all worked up, but this is part of who I am and some of the obligations that go along with business, and I want you to be part of it all with me. So, for now, let's just concentrate on the family dinner in two weeks, and don't worry, everyone will be just as enchanted with you as I am."

He leans over, putting his hand on the back of Cate's seat and touching her hair very gently. "I'd like to kiss you good night now--is that okay?"

Cate's suddenly very nervous with all this talk of making plans for future events. She's starting to think she may have taken this too far already. She doesn't even hear his question.

"Cate, are you okay?"

"Yes. Sorry, I ...."

He leans over and kisses her. Suddenly that's all her mind can focus on. *Damn, why does he have to be so good at this? His kisses could make me forget anything.*

After he helps her get the girls and all their things inside, he stops at the door and kisses her again. This time his kiss is a little more forceful as he presses her back into the door frame. When he pulls away, he just says, "Good night, and thanks for the great day. I'll talk to you tomorrow."

As he walks away she's left breathless, not able to think at all.

Walking to his car, Bill is mentally kicking himself. *Damn it, Sullivan, you pushed too hard. What the hell were you thinking, laying all of that crap on her at one time? You told her it would be at her pace, then you want to throw your whole family on her at once.*

When he gets home, he sulks for a while, then decides he's going to call and apologize and let her know he understands if she's not ready and it's fine.

Cate picks up on the second ring. It sounds like she was sleeping.

He quickly glances at the clock and sees it is 10:30. "Hey, sorry--did I wake you?"

"Not really. I was just starting to doze off. I didn't realize how tired I was until I got the girls to bed and sat for a few minutes."

"Yeah, it was a pretty busy day. Look, I just wanted to call and say I'm sorry for trying to rush things. I get that this is all new to you, and I understand if you're not ready to meet my family. It's okay; we've got plenty of time for that, and as for the dinner thing in Charlotte, that's still weeks away. We'll just see how you feel about that when the time comes, okay?"

"It's okay. I know I panicked when you suggested meeting your family, but I know that if we're going to continue seeing each other, I will have to meet them eventually. I just need a little time to adjust and deal with my fears. If I remember correctly, that's how a relationship progresses. It's just been a really long time for me."

"So, we're okay, then?"

"Yes, we're fine. I just may need a little time to prepare myself for a family meeting."

"Take all the time you need. By the way, that was some kiss you gave me tonight." That makes her laugh; he loves to hear her laugh.

"It certainly was some kiss. You definitely know how to say good night."

Bill feels much better by the time they hang up. He realizes just how deep he's let this woman into his heart. He can't screw this up.

CHAPTER 24

Over the next two weeks, Bill and Cate talk at least once a day and send several instant messages throughout the day, then of course they talk before they go to bed every night and spend the weekends having one adult date and one family outing. A few people at work mention to Cate that they've noticed a difference in her--she seems happier. Her assistant, Julie suspects Cate is seeing someone and tries to hint around for a clue, but Cate isn't giving anything away.

The weekend of Bill's dad's birthday arrives, and she has agreed to go with him, but now that the time is here, she's a bundle of nerves. She hears a car door outside and grabs Phoebe's hand. "Oh God, Mom, he's here. I'm so nervous about meeting his family. Why do I have to meet them all at once?"

Phoebe just smiles and hugs her. "Think of it as pulling off a Band-Aid. You do it quick, all at once, and it's less painful."

She rolls her eyes. "Right."

The doorbell rings just as Cate is getting to the door. She opens it and as usual the butterflies wake up as soon as she sees his smile. She tries to cover her nerves and play it cool. "Hi, come on in. I just have to go tell the girls goodbye--they're in their room playing games."

Bill follows her, so he can say hi to the girls. They're happy to see him; even Shawn has opened up to him and grabs his hand when he walks in. Kaylee immediately asks if he wants to play Candyland with them, but before he can answer, Cate explains they have somewhere to go and maybe he can play with them next time. Kaylee puts on a little pout, but agrees to wait until next time. She takes his other hand as they return to the living room. Cate asks Phoebe if she's sure she'll be okay with the girls until Beth gets there.

Phoebe knows Cate worries about her, but she's gotten so much stronger, she almost feels like her old self again. "Yes, dear; Beth will be here in a few minutes, and she's staying until the girls go to sleep. Everything will be fine--you just go enjoy your evening."

When Cate walks to the bedroom to get her purse, Bill leans over to Phoebe and whispers, "She looks a little nervous; is everything okay?"

Phoebe nods. "She's kind of freaking out over meeting your family."

"I keep telling her they're going to love her."

"She'll be fine--she's just a nervous Nelly."

When Cate returns, Bill takes her hand and kisses it. "You sure you want to do this? It's okay if you don't."

She shakes her head. "No, I'm fine--a little nervous, but fine."

Bill kisses her hand again and turns to Phoebe. "Okay. Phoebe, we'll see you later. Promise I won't keep her out too late."

"Good night, you two. Have fun." Phoebe really likes Bill; she sees how much he cares for Cate and the girls. She's so happy to see Cate coming back to life again.

As they get in the car Bill asks her again, "Are you sure you're doing okay?"

"Yes, just nervous."

He turns to her with a little evil grin. "We can always blow them off and go to my house and make out."

With a little laugh, she says, "Yeah, that would really help give everyone a good first impression of me."

"Hmmm--I don't care about their impressions. I think you're great."

On the drive, they make small talk and she catches him up on things at Sunrise. Soon they turn into a nice upper-class, gated community. They pull in the driveway of a very pretty house and Cate's a little relieved to see that although the house is big, it's not mansion status.

Bill says, "We're a little early, but I wanted you to meet Mom and Dad before the whole gang gets here and bombards you."

She can feel her nerves start to make her stomach jump, so she takes a deep breath, lets it out slowly and says, "Okay, here goes."

Bill walks in the front door without knocking and yells out, "Hey Mom, Dad--we're here."

It only takes a moment for his mom and dad to greet them in the foyer. Bill kisses his mom and hugs his dad, wishing him a happy birthday, and introduces Cate.

Bill's mom hugs her. "Hi, Cate. I'm Marjorie, and this is Bill's dad, Ted. It's so nice to finally meet you."

Ted waits his turn, saying, "Wow, you sure are pretty--come over here and give me a birthday hug."

"Oh, okay, sure. Happy birthday." Cate's fears seem to ease a little as they make her feel welcome. His mom has such a bubbly, warm personality, and his dad looks like an older version of Bill--still very handsome, with that same great smile.

They walk down the hall and it opens into a beautiful open great room with kitchen and dining area. Cate tells Marjorie what a beautiful home they have as she takes it all in.

Marjorie takes Cate's hand and leads her to the kitchen as Bill and his dad follow along. "Thank you. Can I get y'all something to drink?"

Bill steps up. "I'll get it, Mom. Cate, would you like a glass of wine?"

She says yes, and he can see she's still nervous. He brings over a glass and the bottle of wine and pours some for her and refills his mom's glass; he gives her a little kiss on the head and winks at her.

Marjorie was busy preparing the food for the grill and sets back to her work as she turns to Cate. "So, Bill tells me you have two little girls--do you have pictures?"

"I do." She digs her phone out of her purse and brings up the pictures they took at the zoo. "This is Kaylee--she's four--and this is Shawn--she's two."

"Oh, they're just as beautiful as Bill described them." Marjorie smiles at Bill and tells him, "You go help your dad with the grill while I get to know Cate."

He gives his mom a sideways glance, "Mom, no interrogations."

"Don't be silly. Now go."

Once he's out of the room, Marjorie turns to Cate. "I've been dying to meet you--Bill talks about you a lot. I haven't seen him like this since, well, never. He's dated a lot, but you're the first girl he's ever brought home to meet us since high school. He's quite taken with you, and no wonder--you're just beautiful."

Cate is wishing Bill hadn't left her alone so soon. "Oh, thank you."

"Relax, honey--don't be so nervous, we don't bite. Come help me get this stuff ready while we talk."

"Sure. What can I do to help?"

"You can cut up the veggies while I prepare the steaks and chicken. Bill tells me you're a widow. I'm sorry to hear that. It must be difficult being so young with two babies."

Cate starts wondering just how much Bill has told them. "It's been challenging, but my mom has helped a lot."

"That's good. Family is very important."

As they work together in the kitchen, Cate begins to relax a little. Marjorie is really very nice, and she can see how much family means to these people. Suddenly, another voice calls out from the hallway. "Mom, we're here."

Marjorie calls back, "We're in the kitchen," and turns to Cate explaining, "That's Cindy and her gang."

Cate thinks, *Oh boy, just when my nerves were starting to settle down. I think I may need more wine.*

Cindy enters the kitchen with two children trying to push their way past her. "Mom, where do you want me to put the cake?" Then noticing Cate, she smiles. "Oh, hi, you must be Cate, I'm Cindy; this is my husband Kurt and this is Taylor and Emma that are trying to run me over."

Cate rushes over to help. "Hi, very nice to meet you. Do you need some help?"

"Yes, thanks, if you could take the cake and put it wherever Mom says, I have a few more things to get from the car. Where's Dad?"

Just then Bill and Ted come in from the patio. "I'm right here. We thought we heard a tornado blowing through the house."

Cindy laughs as she walks over to kiss her dad and tell him happy birthday. "It's not a tornado yet; wait until TJ gets here with his three boys. Have you heard from them yet?"

Marjorie points to the table where she wants Cate to put the cake while answering Cindy. "Yes, Sherrie called about thirty minutes ago and said they would be here in about an hour, so it shouldn't be long now."

Cindy rolls her eyes. "Right. If she said an hour, it's more like an hour and a half, or two hours. They're always late."

Ted pats Kurt on the back, saying, "Come on, grab a beer and come outside with us so these pretty ladies can chat."

Bill walks over to Cate, gives her another little kiss on the cheek and asks if she's doing okay and if she wants him to stay in kitchen with her.

She smiles, a little embarrassed by his display of affection in front of his mom and sister. "No, I'm fine. Just check on me in a little while."

He squeezes her hand and whispers in her ear, "Okay--and by the way, Mom likes you. She gave me the wink."

About forty-five minutes later, an even louder burst of noise bombards the house as Bill's older brother TJ, his wife Sherrie and their three boys arrive. Cindy was right about a tornado coming through. Cate gets a little twinge of nerves each time someone new comes in, but everyone is very welcoming and has her feeling like she's part of the family before long. After a great dinner and birthday cake and presents, they finally all start saying their good nights and heading out. As Bill and Cate are leaving, Marjorie gives her a hug and says she hopes to see her again soon, and thanks her for putting that sparkle back in her son's eyes.

When they get in the car, Bill reaches over for her hand and asks, "Well, what did you think of my crazy family?"

She squeezes his hand and smiles. "I like them. You all have such a great relationship. That's how I always imagined what having brothers and sisters would be like."

Laughing, he says, "Yeah, they're okay I guess. Believe me, we didn't always get along like that."

"They're not just okay, they're great. Everyone was so nice and really made me feel welcome." She glances over at him with a little grin. "Your mom, Cindy, and Sherrie all said that I'm the first woman you've brought home to meet them."

"You are. I told you, I just never felt the connection with anyone like this before. And, I know it's early, but I'm having a 4th of July barbeque at my house and I'd like y'all to come. All of you, your mom too. We each take turns hosting a holiday. I picked 4th of July because I love the fireworks."

"Oh, well--that sounds great, but that's a couple of months away. Let's see how things go, okay?"

He laughs and shakes his head. "Okay. Hey, is it too soon for me to tell you I'm in love with you?"

Cate, turns her head so quickly that she almost gets whiplash. She's speechless as her mind spins out of control. *WHAT!? Holy crap, the "L" word.* She can't form words. "Oh, I... I--"

He knows he threw her by dropping that on her, so he doesn't wait for her to say anything. "You know, I always heard about love at first sight, but I thought that was all just hype. But Cate, the first day I saw you, I was gone. Now, it's okay if you're not there yet. I just wanted you to know I'm not going anywhere and I'll wait as long as it takes for you to realize you're falling for me too. By the way, that banquet is in three weeks--will you come with me?"

Her head is still spinning. *He says the "L" word, then just switches subjects? I can't think straight.*

"Cate?"

"Oh, what? I--"

"Will you come with me to the banquet in Charlotte?"

She tries to keep up with the change of subject while her mind is still trying to grasp him saying he's falling in love with her. It takes a moment, but she finally catches up with him and decides to pretend he didn't just throw the "L" word out.

"I've been giving that some thought, and Cindy was telling me this is not just some awards banquet. She says you're nominated for Charlotte's Businessman of the Year--that's big. She even offered to take me to a dress shop she knows to buy a dress."

"Wow, so now you're hanging out with my sister?" He seems very pleased and has that smile at its full 1,000 watts of power.

"I guess so. I told her that would be great, because I've never been to anything like that before, so I would really appreciate if she could help me find the right thing to wear."

"So, that's a yes?"

"It's a yes."

"I'm glad you decided to come with me. Thank you."

"Thank you for inviting me."

"No one I'd rather be with. The dinner is Friday night, so why don't you come up Friday morning and I can show you around the town a little?"

"Oh, I don't know. I'll have to check with my boss to see if I can get off."

"Maybe I can put in a good word for you."

They laugh, and Cate feels the knot that's been in her stomach since the "L" bomb start to loosen. "I have to make arrangements for the girls. Maybe I could bring them up with me and they could spend some time with their other grandparents."

"Good idea. I'd like to send a car for you, so you don't have to be on the road alone with the girls, if that's okay?"

"A car? Well, I guess. It's a little weird for me, though."

"I'd feel better, if you don't mind."

"I don't mind. I'm just not used to that. It's just a little weird."

"I want to spoil you and those two little angels. Please let me." Since it seems he's on a roll, he decides to take another chance. "I'd also like if you would consider staying at my place after the dinner. It's going to end pretty late, and the apartment has two bedrooms, so you don't have to worry."

Uh-oh...fear rears its ugly head again, "I don't know...I don't know."

He backs off quickly. "Okay, it's just a suggestion. Think about it."

They stop in front of her house, and Bill thanks her again for going with him to his parents' house. "I was watching you in the kitchen talking to Mom, Cindy, and Sherrie and I kept thinking this is what I've been waiting for. He suddenly turns serious. "I want you in my life; I want to be with you all the time. It kills me all week to be so far away. I can't wait till the weekends to see you. Cate, I don't use the word *love* casually. I meant it when I said I'm in love with you."

Seeing the fear on her face, he reaches up and rubs her cheek so softly, it's barely there. "Please don't get that deer in the headlights look in those beautiful eyes. I'm not expecting you to say anything in return. Not until you're ready. I just want you to know, it's okay to make plans with me because I'm in this for the long haul."

She's not sure how to deal with his declaration of love, but she tries. "Bill, I really enjoy being with you and I look forward to the weekends too. I'm very attracted to you, but I'm just scared. I've had so much happen over the last few years, and it's just been me and my mom against the world trying to raise and protect Kaylee and Shawn from being hurt. I've put up such a wall since Sean's death, and it's not even three years yet. How can I let myself fall for someone else? You make me very happy, but then I feel guilty for being happy. I guess that sounds silly to you, but that's how I feel."

He leans over and hugs her. "It doesn't sound silly at all. It sounds human. Cate, I know Sean was your first love and the two of you shared a life and a love that created those two beautiful girls. I don't want you to forget him, or to diminish what you had. I just want the chance to give you and your girls everything he couldn't. It's okay if I'm not your first love; I just want to be your last."

He releases her a little and brushes back a strand of hair that's fallen into her eyes. "I won't push. I told you we'll go at your pace. I shouldn't have suggested you stay at my place in Charlotte. You're not ready, and that's okay. Just let me hold you and kiss you before you go inside, and I have to go another week without seeing you."

She moves closer to him, and he puts his arms around her and kisses her hair. Cate loves the way he makes her feel; she thanks him for trying to understand.

CHAPTER 25

As the weeks are flying by, Cate and Bill fall into a comfortable routine, and both Kaylee and Shawn have gotten very accustomed to this new arrangement. About mid-week, they start asking where Bill will take them the coming weekend. Kaylee even offers suggestions of where she thinks they should go.

Suddenly, it seems in a blink of an eye it's the day before the awards banquet. Cate's got the perfect dress, shoes, and jewelry thanks to Cindy. Cindy even convinced her to get the matching bra and panties, using the argument that she should do it for herself, to make her feel pretty. She knows Cindy thinks it will be for Bill, but Bill may have to wait to see that.

Cate decides to drive up Thursday afternoon, rather than Friday morning, so she takes off from work a little early to get home to finish packing for herself and the girls. She also asked Phoebe to come with them, since it's been a while since she's had a little getaway. At 4:00, a big black SUV with darkened windows pulls up outside, and there's a knock at the door. When she opens the door, it's the guy who picked Bill up the day of the rainstorm. She's surprised; he seems bigger than she remembered, and she hopes he doesn't remember her.

He introduces himself as Johnny and asks if he can help with her bags. She shakes his hand and introduces herself, her mom, and the girls. He takes the bags to the SUV, and Cate tells him she will have to get the car seats out of her car. All the while she's thinking, *This poor guy's going to think we're moving out*. Johnny informs her as he's opening the back of the SUV that it won't be necessary to get her car seats. Just as she is about to explain that the children can't ride without them, he opens the back door, and she can see the inside is not like a normal SUV; it's more like a limo with a big U-shaped seat to carry several people, and inside are two brand-new car seats. She's speechless.

Once everything is loaded, she buckles the girls in, gives Johnny the address to Debbie and Pat's house, and starts handing out toys and books to get the girls occupied. Johnny lets her know there's a DVD player back there and that Mr. Sullivan had a variety of DVD's in the storage compartment that they may like, and a little tiny refrigerator with drinks if they get thirsty. He then tells her he will raise the privacy screen and if she needs anything to just press a little button on the arm rest in the door.

As the screen starts to rise from behind Johnny's seat, Cate looks at her mom in disbelief. Once the screen is all the way up, they both start to giggle like schoolgirls. They wait about two seconds before they both start opening all the compartments and exploring what's inside. Cate opens the compartment with the DVD's and is blown away to see that it's all Disney movies. She just freezes and can feel the tears welling up in her eyes as she lifts them out to show Phoebe. She just can't believe he would do something so thoughtful. Kaylee immediately starts calling out which movie she wants to watch.

Once Cate figures out how to operate the DVD player and has the movie playing, the girls are entranced, so she sits back to relax. She turns to Phoebe. "Wow, this is nice, huh? I actually get to relax and just enjoy the ride. I'm so glad you decided to come with us, and I think driving up this evening instead of tomorrow morning was a great idea. I really want a chance to talk to Pat and Debbie about me seeing Bill. I hope they won't be upset."

Phoebe just smiles and says, "They won't. I've already told Debbie you were kind of seeing someone. She was actually happy for you."

Cate sits bolt upright in the seat. "What? When?"

"Oh, a couple of months ago. We were talking, and Debbie said you were really sounding good, and I just said that you had been going to dinner with someone."

"What did she say? Why didn't you tell me?"

"She said that it was good, and it was time for you to start living again--and I didn't tell you because it was no big deal, and I knew you would just get all freaked out about nothing. So anyway, it's not going to be a big surprise to them."

She relaxes a bit and sits back in her seat again. "Did she really say it was time I start living again?"

"Yep. Honey, Pat and Debbie love you. They know how much you loved Sean, but they also know he's gone now and you have a whole lifetime ahead of you. They don't want you to be sad and lonely forever. Just make sure you keep them included in things."

"Of course. I will always include them in everything concerning the girls. Well, I guess that kind of takes the pressure off. Thanks, Mom; you're always taking care of me."

"We take care of each other. Can I give you my opinion about something else?"

"Uh-oh...what?"

"Well, you and Bill have been dating for how long now--four or five months? Maybe he's right, you should stay at his place tomorrow after the dinner."

"What?"

"I'm just saying, it might do you some good."

"Mom!"

"Just think about it."

"Mom."

"Cate, when he sees you in that dress he's going to flip. He may not let you leave."

"Mom, stop. Seriously now, I was thinking of asking him to pick me up tomorrow so Pat and Debbie could meet him instead of having a car pick me up. What do you think, is it too soon for them? I don't want to insult them or make them uncomfortable."

"I think you should ask them if they would like to meet him. I think they'll appreciate you wanting their approval."

"I really do want their approval. I don't want to do anything to hurt them or make them think I've forgotten Sean. Because I haven't; I think of him every day."

"I know you do, and he knows it too. The last thing Sean would want is for you to stop living because he had to."

She sighs and glances out of the window. "I know."

CHAPTER 26

After the most relaxing three-hour car ride Cate has ever had, they arrive at the Wilsons'. Debbie and Pat come out of the house as they are getting out of the SUV. They look at the big SUV, then at one another with questioning looks. Debbie rushes over to give everyone hugs; she can't wait to get her hands on Kaylee and Shawn. They miss the girls a lot, and it seems like they grow several inches between visits. When the girls see them, they are just as excited.

Debbie and Pat sweep up the kids and cover them with kisses as Johnny unloads the bags and asks Cate if they will need the car seats. She says no, they already have a set here. She still feels weird about having someone carrying her bags like she's someone important.

Debbie is still gushing over the girls. "Oh, my goodness Kaylee, look how big you're getting. It's only been a month since I've seen you girls, and it looks like you've each grown three inches. I'm so glad to see you! I have a special treat for you. Go inside with Pops and I'll be right in."

As Pat takes the girls inside, Debbie turns to Cate. "Well, it looks like you're moving up in the world, having a car and driver bring you up. Wow, fancy."

They all enter the house and Cate tells Johnny he can just leave the bags there in the living room. She's not sure what to do now; should she tip him? But before she can even blink, he hands her his card and tells her his cell number is on there for her to call if she needs anything, that he is on call for her all weekend. She just stands there looking at his card as he quietly disappears out the door.

When she turns around Debbie and Phoebe are both staring at her. She looks at them, confused, and they all burst out laughing. Debbie puts her arms around Cate and Phoebe and leads them into the kitchen. They sit around the table and catch up while the girls eat the cookies their Maw-Maw made for them.

Debbie finally gets around to asking the question she's been dying to ask. "So, Cate, Phoebe tells me you've started dating someone--tell me all about him."

Cate looks like the cat that ate the canary, she swallows hard before answering, "Yes, his name is Bill Sullivan and we've been sort of dating for a few months now. I hope you're not upset that I didn't tell you before now. I wasn't sure if I was even ready to date, and it just kind of happened."

Smiling, Debbie shakes her head. "No, I'm not upset, but you know you can tell me anything. You're like my own daughter."

Cate can feel the tears stinging her eyes. "I know, but the last thing I would ever want to do is hurt you, or Pat, or to have you think I've forgotten Sean."

Debbie reaches over and takes Cate's hand. "Oh, silly girl, we love you and we know what you and Sean had, and I know if he were still here the two of you would have grown old together. But that wasn't meant to be. Sean was happy every day of his life after he met you. You brought out the very best in my son and put a smile on his face and in his heart. That's what every mother wants for her children. Now, we want to see you with a smile on your beautiful face again, too. So, tell me all about him."

Cate squeezes Debbie's hand. "Well, he's my boss--he owns Sullivan Enterprises. After the acquisition, he started working out of our office during the transition period, and we were working pretty close to each other on a daily basis, and I guess there was some attraction, but it was strictly professional. Then, when I was here for our conference a couple of months ago and we went to dinner that Friday evening, it wound up being just the two of us, and we had a really nice dinner--he's very easy to talk to. Well, then the next week he called and asked me out and we've been seeing each other just about every weekend since. We do a lot of stuff with the girls, and they really like him."

"Oh, honey, I think that's great--as long as he treats you and my munchkins good, that's all that matters. I take it that was his big SUV you came in?"

"Yes. He wanted to make sure we were safe." Now feeling a little braver, Cate asks how they would feel about meeting him.

Debbie and Pat exchange glances, and she nods. "I think we would like that very much."

"Well, tomorrow we have lunch plans, then the awards banquet, and I told him I just wanted a car to pick me up because I wasn't sure how y'all would feel about all of this, but I can tell him it's okay for him to pick me up. If that's okay with you?"

"Well, of course he can pick you up--that way I can give him the once-over, too." Debbie leans over and kisses Cate on the cheek, "Cate, I don't want you to feel like you need our permission to date someone. We all miss Sean, but it's time for you to be happy again."

They hug, and they both have tears in their eyes. Cate wipes away the tear that escaped and is rolling down her cheek. "I appreciate that, but I do care what you and Pat think. You're my family, and I never want to do anything that would hurt either of you."

Debbie wipes away her tears, too. "Honey, your being happy would never hurt us. It will be a little strange to see you with someone else, but you're way too young to not try to find happiness again. Like I said, as long as he's good to you and the girls, we'll be happy for you."

CHAPTER 27

Bill arrives at 10:00 Friday morning to pick Cate up, and he's a little nervous, this is a brand-new situation for him. He's met the parents of girls he's dated in the past, but never their in-laws. However, he knows how important it is to Cate that they feel comfortable with him being a part of their grandchildren's lives. He understands these people will be a part of his life too, if things work out the way he hopes.

Cate answers the door when he rings the bell and invites him in. He's glad they're not all standing in the living room waiting to meet him as soon as he walks in. He gives Cate a little kiss and takes in her beauty, wondering again how he got so lucky. He follows her into the den and can't help but watch her walk and admire how well her jeans fit.

Cate introduces him to Pat and Debbie, and the girls light up when they see him. Kaylee immediately starts telling Bill all about the zoo she and Shawn are building out of Duplo blocks. Finally, Cate has to distract her so Bill can talk to Pat and Debbie. They ask the usual questions about his company and where he lives, and he explains that he divides his time between Charlotte and Charleston and tells them a little about his family. About a half hour later, Cate and Bill are on their way to lunch.

When they get in his car, that same little MG he was driving the day of the rainstorm, he takes Cate's hand, kisses it, and says, "Well, I think that went well--they're very nice people, and I hope this will help you feel a little better about dating me."

Cate realizes she does feel a little better. "They are nice people, and I just don't want to hurt them."

"I know; that's one of the things I love about you. You always put others before yourself. You're a good person, Cate Wilson."

"Thanks. I think you are, too." Before things start getting too mushy, she asks where they're going for lunch.

He glances over and gives her that killer smile. "I rented a boat for the afternoon, and we're going to cruise around the lake and have lunch."

Cate raises her eyebrows in surprise. "Well, that's certainly different--sounds nice and relaxing, and it's a beautiful day for it."

He glances over at her with a concerned look. "I was thinking on the way over that maybe I should have told you of the plans first, just in case you get seasick or hate boats."

Laughing, she says, "I don't hate boats, and I don't think I get seasick. I've never really been on many boats, but I'm sure it will be fine."

A few minutes later they pull into the marina. "Here we are--it's the blue and white one over there."

She can't hide the shocked look on her face. "That one? That's not a boat, it's a yacht. Who else is coming?"

He loves surprising her. "No one; just us." He jumps out and rushes around to open her door. Cate just sits there for a minute thinking, *This is crazy. I mean, how much money does this guy have, that he can rent something like this for the afternoon?*

Bill reaches in and takes her hand, and leads her down the dock to the stairs leading up to the biggest boat she's ever seen up close. As they reach the top step, he tells her they have to take their shoes off before boarding.

She reaches down and slips her shoes off and puts them in a little box there on the deck next to Bill's shoes. One of the men standing on the deck hands them a new pair of shoes to slip on. Cate takes her shoes and turns to Bill still in awe, saying, "Wow, this is gorgeous."

The older man introduces himself. "Hello, Mr. Sullivan, I'm Martin your captain for today--and this is Lance, your chef, and Brad, your server. May we start you both off with something to drink and a tour of the *Lady D*?"

Bill shakes the captain's outstretched hand. "Yes, that would be great. Two glasses of white wine, please." He turns back to Cate and asks if she's okay.

She feels like she's in a dream. "Yes, just amazed--this is beautiful."

As they turn to follow the captain, Bill takes her hand and kisses it again. "I love seeing your eyes sparkle like that. You are so beautiful."

After the full tour, the captain returns to the bridge and they slowly move away from the dock. Bill brings her to the rail and puts his arms around her, just breathing her in. He can't believe the effect this woman has on him. They stay like that until they are well out on the lake when Brad approaches announcing that lunch will be ready in a few minutes and asks if they would like more wine.

They sit at a romantic table for two on the deck and sip their wine as lunch is served. Cate is having a hard time believing this is real. It all feels like a dream. Things like this don't happen to girls like her--this is stuff you see in the movies. While they cruise around the lake, Bill points out different points of interest and tells her a little history on each.

Cate can't help but wonder how many other women he's taken on this same cruise. She thinks he must have done this many times to know all the history of the places around the lake the way he does.

He notices she's suddenly become quiet, so he changes the subject. "Lunch was great; I hope you enjoyed it. This is so nice, so relaxing and peaceful just cruising around the lake. I love having this private time with you." Turning his head so he can look in her eyes, he asks, "Is everything okay? You're being so quiet."

"Yes, I'm fine. I was just thinking that you must have spent a lot of time on this lake to know all this history the way you do."

"I have. We've booked lake tours several times for business gatherings. Never on a vessel this nice, usually on one of the tour boats. I must have heard the lake history at least a dozen times over the years. I was trying to impress you with my amazing knowledge--did it work?"

Cate laughs and is surprised by the feeling of relief that just washed over her. "Yes, I'm very impressed." She glances down at her hands and admits she thought for a moment that this may have been a standard date destination. Bill lifts her chin and kisses her gently on her lips. "Silly girl, I would never take you to a standard date destination, if I actually had one. There is nothing standard about what I feel for you."

Cate blushes a little and asks, "Why are you so good to me?"

"That's a silly question. I told you--I'm in love with you. Making you smile makes me happy."

Uneasy about looking directly in his eyes, she glances out at the lake and asks, "How do you know it's love? Maybe it's just infatuation."

He gets up from the table and leads her to the cushioned seating area around the back of the deck and pulls her down next to him. "Cate, I've been infatuated with women before; what I feel for you, and have since that first day I saw you, is something I've never felt before, and the more I get to know you, the stronger it gets." He rubs his finger over her forehead. "You're furrowing your brow-- what are you thinking?"

She brings her free hand up and brushes it across her forehead to remove the furrow. "I don't know. It would be so easy to just let myself go and fall in love with you too. Maybe I already have, but I'm scared. It's not just me involved here."

He pulls back suddenly. "Wait, did you say you've fallen in love with me too?"

She loves that he always makes her laugh. "Ha-ha, I said maybe."

Looking quite satisfied, he says, "That's good enough for now. I know you're scared, and I'm well aware that this is a package deal, but I'm in love with all three of you. I want nothing more than to help you raise Kaylee and Shawn. The more time I spend with the three of you, the more I want it full time. I finally feel like my life is complete."

As she listens to him she thinks, *Being with him is so easy. When he holds me, and kisses me like this, I never want it to stop. Maybe I should just stop thinking so much and just go with my feelings. I want him, all of him, so much. Oh, please God, let this be real.*

They sit cuddled together on the cushions, watching the other boats and the seagulls soaring and diving and just enjoying being close. Bill hates it, but he breaks the silence. "Ahh, back at the dock already. I hope you enjoyed our afternoon as much as I did."

Cate wishes the peaceful feeling she's been enjoying could go on forever, as she nods in agreement. "I did--this was fantastic." Walking back to the car hand-in-hand, she asks what time he's picking her up for the dinner.

He opens the door for her, and says, "Drinks start at 7, dinner is for 8, so I'll pick you up about 6:30, if that's okay?"

She glances at her watch and notices it's already a little after 3:00. "Sure, I'll be ready. I can't wait to see you in a tux."

"Ha-ha, and I can't wait to see you in your dress. Cindy said I was going to be blown away, but I'm blown away by you in jeans, so if it gets any better it may kill me."

"We'll have to wait and see, won't we?

CHAPTER 28

Cate's nerves start to kick in as she puts on the finishing touches. Even though she thinks they've done a pretty good job of keeping their relationship away from work, she knows tonight the people that work closest with Bill will be there, but he says they already know about them and nothing has come out so far, so maybe she's worrying for nothing.

She stands back checking herself in the mirror for the hundredth time, even she has to admit that this dress is fabulous. The emerald green of the dress makes her eyes really stand out, and she really likes the look of the just barely off the shoulder angle of the neckline, combined with Debbie's fantastic job on her hair with the up-do, and her mom's pearls added just the right touch of elegance. Cindy was right; the matching emerald-green bra and panties with the black lace overlay do make her feel pretty. She checks her hair one more time, thinking, *I'll have to thank Cindy again for helping me pick everything. I haven't felt this pretty in forever.*

When she walks into the living room everyone stops and looks at her. Phoebe walks over and hugs her. "Oh, Cate, you look absolutely stunning."

Everyone agrees. Kaylee even tells her, "Mommy, you look so beautiful--just like a princess."

Cate bends down and gives Kaylee and Shawn both kisses, then looks to Phoebe and Debbie. "Do you really think I look okay?"

Pat chimes in, "Okay? You'll probably win the award for the most beautiful woman there. Hell, Bill will probably win just for being with you. Speaking of Bill, a big black limo just pulled up outside. I assume that's him."

Suddenly, another wave of nerves washes over her. "A limo? Oh, I didn't know we were going in a limo."

Debbie laughs. "Honey, you're in the big time now. I'll get the door."

When she opens the door, Debbie is struck by how incredibly handsome Bill looks. When she met him this morning she thought he was handsome, but wow, in a tuxedo he's gorgeous.

Bill stands at the door waiting to be invited in. "Hi Debbie, good to see you again."

"Oh, sorry, please come on in. Don't you look handsome?"

When Bill enters the living room, he is absolutely awestruck. "WOW! I'm speechless. WOW!" All he can think is, *My God, this woman is beautiful. I don't think I can be a good boy any longer. As beautiful as she is in that dress, it only makes me want to get her out of it more.*

Cate laughs and is equally as impressed with how good he looks in a tux. "Wow, yourself." She can feel the heat rising all the way from her toes. *Holy hell, he's so good-looking. I never really thought about a man in a tux, but this image is burned into my memory forever.*

Phoebe jumps up with phone in hand. "Hold on--I want to get a picture of you two."

Cate rolls her eyes. "Mom, please—I'm not going to the prom."

"I don't care—y'all both look too good not to capture it. It will only take a second."

Bill just laughs. "No problem, Phoebe. Send me a copy too."

As they walk to the car with the driver waiting, holding the door open, Cate does feel like a princess and wonders if she can get used to Bill's lifestyle. Once inside, Bill pours them each a glass of champagne. Cate accepts her glass and muses aloud, "I wasn't expecting a limo."

Bill just smiles. "It's all first class for you, doll."

Cate wonders if he's aware of the effect that smile has on women; then she quickly tries to move her mind in a different direction. "I've never been to anything like this before, so tell me what to expect."

They relax back into the very comfortable seats and before answering her question, Bill just stares at her for a few awkwardly silent seconds. He reaches up and brushes her exposed neck with his fingertips, causing a little shiver to run down her spine.

He tells her, "You are so beautiful. I can't believe how lucky I am." When she blushes, and looks down at her hands, he turns to answering her question. "Well, when we get there, there'll be a few members of the press; they'll be taking pictures and looking for a statement from each of the nominees."

She feels the blood drain from her face. "Press? Does that mean our pictures will be in the paper?"

"Probably."

Now she's really nervous. "Well so much for keeping this quiet and away from work."

Bill reaches over and lifts her chin to make her look at him. "Don't be nervous--it won't be a bad as you think. This stuff gets buried in the society pages, and no one looks at that anyway. Besides, we can't keep us secret forever."

Still looking into his enchanting blue eyes, she has trouble focusing. “I know, but it just makes me nervous.”

He gives her a little light kiss on the lips. “I promise it won’t be bad; we’ll move so quick, we’ll just be a blur.” This makes her laugh. So he continues, “Once inside we’ll do a little mingling, and I’ll have the pleasure of introducing you around and watching everyone wonder how the hell I landed such a beautiful woman. Every guy there will be envious.”

She just rolls her eyes. “Right, I’m sure they’re quite used to you being seen with beautiful women.”

He holds up his index finger. “Ahh, there’s superficial beauty; then there’s true beauty, and that’s what you have. Once you are officially introduced to everyone that matters, we’ll take our seats and they’ll serve dinner and talk up each of the nominees and announce this year’s winner.

“After that, whoever wins will have to give an acceptance speech then more pictures, and then it all moves into the ballroom for drinks and dancing. That’s the part I’m waiting for. I can’t wait to get you on the dance floor and hold you close.”

She laughs again and takes another sip of champagne. “I like that thought. So, who else will be at our table?”

“Just family at our table--TJ and Sherrie, Cindy and Kurt, and Mom and Dad. My second table will have a few close friends.”

She feels a little relieved. “Oh, great. I was worried I wouldn’t know anyone. That makes me feel a lot better. Who will be there from the office?”

“Ed and Laura will be there.”

“Do they know about us already?”

“Yes. Ed figured me out pretty quick when we went in after the acquisition. He saw right away the way I looked at you, and Laura—well, there's no keeping anything from her. She's like my second mother."

The limo slows down and pulls in line to let them out. "Well, this is it; looks like we're here. Don't worry--I won't leave you alone."

She grips his hand tighter and takes a deep breath. "Good. Please don't."

CHAPTER 29

When they get out of the car, it's not as bad as she imagined. There's only a few members of the press with their photographers. She envisioned a scene like on TV when movie stars walk the red carpet.

Bill stops for a couple of questions about the nomination; then one young reporter asks Bill to introduce his date for the evening. He glances over at Cate and winks before saying, "This is the love of my life." Then he turns away and pulls her by the hand through the doors. Once inside he turns to her and asks, "You okay?"

She's stunned by his answer. "The 'Love of Your Life'?"

"Yeah, that's what you are, and I didn't think you wanted your name printed in the paper. I noticed that the photographers, being male, were loving you, which of course I don't blame them for--I do too. After all, you look like you just stepped off the cover of a magazine. How about a glass of champagne, then we can mingle a little?"

She's still trying to grasp the "LOVE OF MY LIFE" thing as she numbly answers, "Champagne would be great."

As they walk to the bar, every man they pass turns to admire her. She seems oblivious to it, but it does not go unnoticed by Bill.

When they reach the bar, a very beautiful tall blonde woman in a skin-tight red dress cut very low in the front and even lower in the back walks up and runs her hand down Bill's arm. "Bill, darling, how have you been? I haven't seen you around lately."

Bill looks at her, not even the slightest bit interested in all the exposed skin. "Selena, I've been fine. Let me introduce you to Catherine Wilson. Cate, Selena Montgomery."

Selena turns to Cate, visibly measuring her up. "Oh, nice to meet you. Do you prefer Catherine, or Cate?"

Cate shakes her hand, quietly wondering just how well this woman knows Bill. "Cate is fine; nice to meet you too."

Selena quickly dismisses Cate and turns her attention back to Bill, rubbing her hand up and down his arm. "You look so handsome. I always loved seeing you in a tux."

Bill moves his arm and puts it around Cate's waist. "So, Selena, who are you with this evening?"

She casts her eyes between the two of them. "I'm with one of your co-nominees, Mitch Honeycutt. We've been seeing each other for a while now."

Bill gives a little laugh. "Well, congratulations." Anxious to end this conversation, Bill says, "Excuse us--I see some of my party has arrived."

Selena, never one to give up easily when there's something she wants, smiles and touches Bill's other arm. "Sure, we'll talk later." Then she turns and walks away with the sexiest walk Cate has ever seen.

Once she's out of earshot, Cate looks at Bill. "That seemed little tense."

Bill takes their drinks from the bar, hands Cate hers, and shakes his head. "Sorry about that. I dated Selena a few times."

That was quite evident to Cate, and she's surprised that she feels a little twinge of jealously. "Oh, well--she's very pretty. She looks like a model."

Bill looks into Cate's sparkling green eyes and gives her

a little smile. "She is a model, but it's all outward beauty, believe me."

Before he can explain any further, a very handsome older man walks up and slaps Bill on the back. "Bill, good to see you. Congrats on the nomination again this year--and who is this lovely lady?"

Bill turns and shakes his hand. "Thank you, Mr. Mayor. This lovely lady is Cate Wilson."

The mayor shakes Cate's hand, "Ms. Wilson, very nice to meet you."

Cate is thoroughly impressed; she's never even been in the same building as a mayor, much less shaking hands with one. "Thank you, sir. A pleasure to meet you too."

As the mayor turns to go, he slaps Bill on the back again and says, "You don't need any more awards when you have this beautiful lady by your side. Cate, maybe you could save a dance for me later."

Bill laughs. "I know, I feel like the luckiest guy in this place."

When he walks away, Cate turns to him and mouths, "Wow, the mayor?"

"Yeah, he's a good guy. I've known him a long time, but he has another thought coming if he thinks he's getting a dance with you."

They continue to mingle around the room, and Cate is continually impressed with the people attending and how well Bill knows them. Bill's family and friends arrive, and they walk over to greet them. Everyone hugs Bill, congratulating him, and they turn to Cate and hug her too, letting her know they are happy she's here for him. Of course, they are all quite sure that this is his year to win.

By the time everyone gets a drink, people are starting to make their way to the dining room. As they turn to go,

Bill notices Laura and Ed coming in. He catches Cate's hand. "There's Laura and Ed--I'm going to catch them. Do you want to come with me or go to the table with Mom?"

She's feeling a lot more comfortable now and is happy that his family is there, so she says she'll go to the table with them. Before letting go of her hand, Bill looks deep into her eyes. "Have I told you in the last five minutes how beautiful you are?"

She just laughs. "Ha-ha, you're crazy. See you at the table."

Bill starts making his way through the crowd filing in to the dining room when he hears someone calling his name. "Bill, Bill-- wait."

When he turns, Selena is right on his heels. "Selena, shouldn't you be at the table with your date?"

Not being easily deterred, she answers, "Shouldn't you? Bill, I just wanted to say that I've missed you; maybe we could get together for a drink sometime." She runs one finger down his lapel. "I remember how much fun an evening of drinks and dancing--and afterward--was with you."

She starts to reach for his face, and he grabs her hand before she can touch him. "I thought you were with Honeycutt now."

She just laughs. "I am, but I can always make time for you."

Not being the least bit interested, he says, "Well, thanks, but I'm with Cate now, and only Cate."

Selena puts on her best sexy pout. "Hmmm, sounds serious. I've never heard you say you were with anyone exclusively before."

Bill turns to go. "I am now."

Selena is not used to a man rejecting her; she just smiles. "Well, you have my number when you get bored with Suzie Sunshine and want some real fun."

Bill just nods. "Later, Selena. Gotta go."

As he turns, Laura and Ed are approaching him. He shakes Ed's hand and gives Laura a hug. "Glad you could both make it."

Without missing a beat, Laura asks, "Was that Selena you were talking to?"

Bill shakes his head. "Yeah, she cornered me."

Before he can say more, Laura says, "You know that woman is nothing but trouble. You better not mess up the good thing you have with Cate."

Bill puts up both hands. "Calm down, Mama Laura--I have no intention of messing anything up with Cate, especially not with someone like Selena."

Satisfied, Laura smiles at him. "Good. Now, where is that lovely young lady?"

"She's at the table with my folks." As they head into the dining room, most of the tables are filling up. Bill gets stopped several times along the way as friends and acquaintances wish him well.

Cate is feeling very comfortable now that Bill's family is there and the conversation at the table is light and relaxed. She thinks, *This is really nice--I love watching Bill interacting with everyone. He's so confident and at ease, and SOOO hot in that tux. I can't keep my eyes off of him. I know he sees it, because he keeps smiling every time he looks at me, and his eyes get just a little deeper blue, and it feels like he's reading my mind. I guess after this weekend everyone at work will know we're dating, but I'll just have to deal with it as it comes.*

He finally returns to their table and takes Cate's hand. "You're all smiles for someone who was so nervous a couple of hours ago."

She leans closer to him so he can hear her over the crowd. "It's funny, I'm really not nervous at all now. I've been watching you and enjoying the view."

He raises his eyebrows. "Really? Well, when this is over we can go back to my place and you can get a better view. What do you think?"

Laughing, she says, "I think I'll take that into consideration and get back to you."

Now he laughs. "Spoken like a true businesswoman."

After a wonderful dinner, several drinks, and an hour of talking up each nominee, the head of the Charlotte Chamber of Commerce finally gets to the big announcement. "This year's Charlotte Chamber of Commerce Businessperson of the year is...Mr. William Sullivan of Sullivan Enterprises."

The table goes wild, and everyone is cheering and clapping and congratulating Bill as he walks up to the podium. Cate is so happy for him and so proud. He acts like it's no big deal, but she knows it's a huge honor. Bill walks up to the podium looking so hot and sexy and flashes that gorgeous smile at everyone, then looks right at Cate and winks at her. She smiles, thinking, *Damn, I'm in love with him and I think I may take him up on that offer of getting a better view of him.*

CHAPTER 30

After Bill's acceptance speech, photos, and all the congratulations from his family, friends, and what seems like everyone else in attendance, they finally make their way to the dance floor where a great little jazz band is playing. Bill finally gets Cate in his arms and pulls her very close to him. He nuzzles her bare neck, sending shivers down her spine, and whispers in her ear how good it feels to hold her so close. Cate is in total agreement with how good it feels, but only says, "Hmmm, you're a very good dancer, Mr. Sullivan."

He runs his hand down her back. "Thank you, Ms. Wilson. It's easy when you have someone you love in your arms."

She smiles and puts her head down on his shoulder, "Yes, it is."

In total surprise, Bill replies, "Why, Ms. Wilson, that's the second time today that you've alluded to the fact that you just may be falling in love with me. I like it."

They both laugh, and as one song turns into another, they never leave the dance floor.

Cate finally asks if they can take a little break so she can visit the little girls' room. He reluctantly agrees, but warns her they are not finished. When they get back to their table she grabs her purse, and Bill asks what she would like to drink. She tells him she only wants water--she wants to keep her senses about her--and she heads toward the ladies' room.

While Bill is asking the waiter for their drinks, Ed walks up. "Bill, congratulations again on the award."

"Thanks, Ed. Can I get you a drink?"

"No, getting ready to head out. Looks like things are getting serious with you and Cate."

Bill nods. "Yeah, they are. I think I finally found The One."

Not surprised, Ed slaps him on the back. "That's great. I'm really happy for you. She's a lovely young woman, but before you do anything rash, let's sit down and start an outline for a pre-nup."

That was the last thing Bill was expecting. "Pre-nup? Ed, we're not getting married tomorrow." Even though the thought of asking her has crossed his mind, he just doesn't want to scare her away by asking too soon. But a pre-nup? He doesn't think they're ready for that yet.

Ed just nods. "Bill, you pay me to look out for your and Sullivan Enterprises' best interests. Trust me, it will be easier if we start talking about this now."

Bill just shakes his head. "Let's talk about it next week."

Ed agrees, "Okay, well, I'm heading out. Have a good night."

"You too, thanks for coming." Bill hadn't even thought of needing a pre-nup; now Ed has his mind wondering how to even broach a subject like that.

As Cate is making her way across the room, Laura catches up with her. "Are you heading to the ladies' room?"

Cate really likes her; she can tell Laura cares a lot for Bill and she knows how much Bill trusts her with everything. "Yeah, I think Bill's trying to dance my feet off."

"I'll walk with you. I must say, you two look so good together. It just warms my heart to see Bill so happy.

I've worked with him for a long time, from the start of Sullivan Enterprises, and I've never seen him happier."

It makes Cate feel good to know she's making him happy. "He's really a great guy. I keep asking myself how I got so lucky."

Laura nods. "Honey, I think he's just as lucky as you are. Don't discount yourself."

When they pass the last table before the restrooms, someone calls out to Laura. She turns to see an old business acquaintance of Bill's. "Oh, Dwight--hi. How have you been?" She turns to Cate. "Excuse me just a minute. I must go say hi to Dwight. I'll catch up with you."

"Okay." When she gets to the ladies' room, she takes a quick glance at her reflection in the mirror, and is surprised at how good she looks and thinks, *Wow, what a great day. I could get used to this.* She's happy to see that the stalls are private little rooms and quite roomy, but she still struggles with her dress and laughs to herself. *Whoever invented evening gowns did not put much thought into the probability that a lady may have to use the bathroom at some point.*

Selena catches sight of Cate going into the ladies' room and quickly grabs her friend Rachel. "Take a walk with me to the restroom."

Rachel looks at her a little strangely. "Sure, Selena. What's going on?"

Selena nods her head toward the ladies' room. "Suzie Sunshine just went in there, and I just want to plant a few seeds in her head."

Rachel rolls her eyes. "Selena, leave it alone--you're with Mitch now."

Selena just laughs, "Mitch, right. If he wasn't so damn rich, do you really think I'd be with a 75-year-old? Okay, follow my lead."

As they enter the restroom, Selena acts like they are in the middle of a conversation. She's glad no one else is in there except the restroom attendant, who Selena does not even consider a person. "Rach, you look great tonight. I love your dress."

Rachel decides it's better to go along than to try to talk her out of something she has her mind set on. "Thanks, Selena. You look great, too. I haven't seen you and Mitch on the dance floor very much tonight."

"No, his knees are bothering him; that's the downfall of dating an older man."

Rachel knows the drill; she and Selena have been friends for a long time so she continues with the plan. "Did you see Bill and his new girlfriend? I don't think they sat out one dance."

Selena raises her voice just a little to make sure Cate can hear them. "Oh yeah, I saw, but that's okay; he and I talked earlier about how much fun we used to have. He asked me to text him my phone number."

Rachel's into it now. "Really? I thought he was all into the new girl."

"I guess he just wants to keep his options open. Besides, from what I hear, she works for him. She's a widow, or divorced, or something, with a few kids, and you know what a knight in shining armor he is for a damsel in distress. I mean really, can you imagine Bill Sullivan, the ultimate bachelor, tied down to a woman with a couple of kids that aren't even his?"

Rachel is primping in the mirror. "Are you sure you're not just jealous?"

"Well, maybe a little, but I think he'll come to his senses soon. I mean, Bill playing daddy, right? That can't last long."

Before she can elaborate any further, Laura enters the restroom. "Oh, Laura, how are you?"

Laura just glances at her. “Selena.”

Selena’s not quite finished getting in her digs. “Looks like Bill took pity on several of his employees tonight.”

Laura never liked this girl from the first time she met her. She could see right through her and Selena knew it, so she didn’t care much for Laura either.

“Oh, Selena, you would think that--because you’re such a shallow person, you wouldn’t know what it’s like to really care for anyone. You’re actually pretty pathetic.”

“Right, I’m pathetic. I’m with one of the richest men in the country and you’re still just ekeing along, taking whatever scraps Bill will throw your way. I’m sure you’re just dying for the day he would ever see you as more than a mere employee.”

“Oh, Selena, grow up. Some people are capable of genuinely caring for others without wanting anything in return.”

Selena just rolls her eyes and heads for the door. “Right. You take care now.”

Once she exits, Laura says quietly to herself, “Ugh, that witch. I’d like to strangle her.” Just then she sees one of the stall doors open and Cate comes out looking very pale. “Oh, Cate, I didn’t think you were still in here. Are you okay? Did that witch tell you something?”

Cate can barely contain the tears. “No, I don’t think she even knew I was in here.”

Laura puts her arm around Cate’s shoulder. “Honey, you look like you’re about to cry. What happened? What did she say?”

Cate just washes her hands and tries to pull it together. “Nothing, I’ve got to go.”

CHAPTER 31

Cate holds her head high as she walks back to their table. She doesn't look left or right, but this doesn't keep her from catching a glimpse of Selena's evil smile in her peripheral vision as she passes their table.

When she reaches her table, Bill can tell something's wrong. "Hey Babe, I was getting worried. You okay?"

She can barely look at him, much less speak to him as she fights back the tears that want to flow. "I'm fine."

He takes her hand. "Ready to dance a little more?"

She gently takes her hand back. "No, I think I'd like to rest my feet a little. Why don't you dance with your mom and Laura? I think they've been waiting all night for a dance."

It's plain to see the difference in her mood. "Are you okay? Did something happen?"

She picks up her glass of water and sips, trying to wash away the lump in her throat. "I'm fine, I just need a break."

Before he can ask again, Bill's mom walks up and asks him for a dance before they leave. Bill takes his mother's hand. "Yeah, sure." He looks at Cate, concerned. "I'll be right back."

As they walk away, Bill's dad sits down next to Cate. "Whew, some night, huh?"

She wants to run, but tries her best to sound like everything is fine. "Oh, yes--some night."

Ted doesn't seem to notice that she's silently dying sitting there. "Marjorie had to have a dance with Bill before we leave. When we were your age, we would dance all night, just like you two. I see a lot of what Marjorie and I have in you and Bill. I've never seen my boy so happy. You're good for him, Cate."

Well, that almost pushes her over the edge, but she manages to get out a polite "thank you." Then Ted looks at her. "You doing okay?"

She nods and tries to play it off. "Yes, I'm fine, just getting a little tired. I'm not used to such late evenings."

He laughs. "Me either, anymore. Ahh, here they come." He turns to Marjorie. "Now, can we go? I'm old and need my rest."

Marjorie pats his arm. "Yes, dear." Then she turns to Bill. "Honey, congratulations again--and Cate, it's been so good seeing you again. Hope to see you soon."

Cate manages a little smile. "Thank you. Good night." Bill kisses his mom and shakes his dad's hand again and tells them good night and thanks them again for coming. The rest of his family seem to magically appear as they all start saying their goodbyes.

Once everyone walks away, Bill turns to Cate. "Hey, what's going on? Tell me what happened."

Cate glances down at her hands. "Nothing happened. I'm just getting tired."

Before he can say anything else, Laura walks up. "Bill, got a minute for a quick dance for your second mom before I leave?" He glances at Cate and she fakes a smile and nods her approval.

When they get on the dance floor, Bill tells Laura, "I don't know what's up. Everything was great, then Cate went to the ladies' room and now she seems upset, but she keeps saying everything is fine. I may not be an expert on women, but I know enough to know when they say 'I'm fine,' things are not fine."

Laura shakes her head. "Well, I'm not really sure what happened, but I walked in on Selena and her friend in the restroom, and of course she had a few snide comments for me about you bringing all of your employees here tonight. After they left, Cate came out of the stall and looked like she was ready to cry. I'm not sure what else was said, but I'm sure that witch had something to do with it."

Bill gives Laura a kiss on the head. "Laura, I love you. You're always on top of everything."

She just laughs. "That's why you pay me the big bucks."

After their dance, she says her good nights and gives Cate a hug. Bill thanks her again for coming and gives her a kiss on the cheek. As she leaves, Bill turns to Cate. "Have your feet rested enough? Are you ready to hit the dance floor again?"

She just shakes her head. "No, I think I would really like to go now, if you don't mind. I mean, you don't have to leave--I understand if you have to stay, but I would really like to have the car take me home."

"Okay, we can leave if that's what you want." She glances up at him. "But what about your obligations here?"

"I'm not obligated to stay. Besides, looks like the crowd is thinning anyway. I'll call for the car to be brought around."

Cate doesn't know how much longer she can hold her composure. "Look, I don't want to ruin your evening just because I'm ready to leave."

"You're not ruining anything. I've had a fantastic evening with you. If you're tired, we'll leave."

She glances down at her hands again. "Okay."

When they get settled in the back of the limo, Bill pushes the button to raise the privacy screen. “Now that we’re alone, are you going to tell me what happened back there? I know something happened, because everything was great, and then when you got back from the ladies’ room you barely wanted to look at me. Cate, please tell me what happened.”

Cate doesn’t want to look him in those gorgeous eyes; she knows she won’t be able to stay strong if she does. “Nothing happened; I guess I just had a reality check. You and I are from different worlds. I have two children, and you have no idea how that would change your life, and I can’t risk opening my and my children’s lives up to something that will never work.”

He’s dumbfounded by her answer. “Cate, what the hell are you talking about? I know having kids is a life-changing experience. I’ve seen my brother and sister, and just about all of my friends go through it. I’m not afraid of that. Hell, it’s what I want more than anything. I want you and your kids in my life forever. I want you to change my life. I love you and those girls. I’ve told you before, if anyone stands to get their heart broken in this, it’s me. I knew from the very beginning that I wanted to be a family with you and Kaylee and Shawn, and the more I’m with you, the more I know this is right. Tell me what she said.”

This time she does look at him. “Who?”

“Selena. Laura told me she thought Selena said something to upset you.”

Cate isn’t sure whether to be annoyed or relieved that Laura told Bill about the incident. “She didn’t say anything to me. She didn’t even know I was there.”

He takes her hand in his and tilts her chin up to make her look at him. “Then what did she do--what happened?”

She notices they are pulling up in front of Bill's apartment building. "Why are we here at your apartment? I told you I wanted to go home."

She starts to pull her hand away, but he holds tight. I'll take you back to Pat and Debbie's if that's what you want, but first we're going upstairs and sort this out. I'm not ending this fantastic night with things like this."

They don't speak all the way up to his penthouse. Once inside, Bill heads to the kitchen. "I'm going to fix us a cup of coffee and we're going to hash this out."

She stands in the living room, not knowing what to do. "Bill, really, there is nothing to hash out. I'm just tired and want to go home."

He comes back to her and takes both her hands and kisses her softly on the cheek. "Cate, I may not be the smartest guy in the world, but I know you don't go from laughing and having a great time to serious and looking like you want to cry in ten minutes without something happening. I want a relationship with you. I want a life with you, and if we're going to have that, we have to talk about things, everything, good and bad."

She searches his eyes trying to decide if he's being sincere, thinking, *He's right--even if I decide this won't work, he does deserve to know why.* She takes a deep breath as they walk hand in hand into the kitchen, and suddenly it just all starts to pour out.

"Okay, you're right, but Selena didn't say anything to me. I was in the stall when she and her friend came in. They started talking about you, and she seemed to know that I was widowed and had two kids. I don't know how she knew anything about me, but she was laughing about you being tied down to someone with two kids that aren't even yours and saying you like to be the knight in shining armor and save the damsel in distress. That once you realized how difficult it would be, you would be moving on as usual. She also said the two of you talked and you asked her for her number because you wanted to keep your options open."

As she finishes her last sentence, she sees his eyes go from that beautiful bright blue to almost black. She stops talking and there is silence for what feels like minutes, but she knows it was only a few seconds. Bill feels the anger rise up in his chest; all he can think is *I'll destroy that bitch.* He has to wait a few seconds before he can speak to Cate like a rational person. He just says, "And you bought all of that?"

She's a little nervous with the change she sees in him. "No...I don't know. Nothing she said was anything I hadn't already thought on my own. I guess hearing someone else verbalize it just made it real. Then when she said you asked for her number, that hurt more than anything else."

He takes her hand again and kisses it. "Oh, Cate--first of all, I never asked Selena for her number. She approached me when I was getting our drinks and tried to stir up conversation. I was polite but did not engage her. She offered her number, but I was not interested and told her I was in a relationship. She said she was too, but we could still have fun. I told her I was not interested. That was it.

"As for suggesting she knows anything about me and what I want for my life, she doesn't know me at all. Let me tell you all there is about me and Selena."

He tilts her chin up again to make her meet his eyes. "We met one night at a bar. I was out with some business associates for drinks and she was there with some people I know. They introduced us, we talked--she's an attractive woman, and we spent the night together. We each had some social engagements coming up over the next couple of months that we went to together. We dated a total of four or five times. It was very casual dating and sex, that's it.

"After about the third date, I knew she was not someone I wanted to be with. I only dated her again because I had already committed myself. We didn't even sleep together the last time we went out; I wasn't interested. She called me a few times after that, but I told her I was too busy--that was it. Yeah, we slept together, but it was nothing more than sex. Cate, she's a shallow, jealous person who only uses people to get what she wants, and I guess she's pissed because she couldn't use me."

Cate's not sure what to think, but in all the time she's known Bill she's never known him to lie, so she makes the decision to believe him over someone she's never met before. "That's it? You only dated a few times?"

"That's it. I swear to you."

"She certainly made it sound like she knew you much better than that."

"Of course she did. She knew you were in there, and she wanted to hurt you and try to break us up."

"Do you really think she knew I was there? Why would she want to break us up? That just doesn't make sense to me."

"Of course she knew. She doesn't do anything by accident. She's very calculating. Selena's the type of person that thinks she can get whatever she wants, and when she doesn't, she gets very vindictive."

Cate feels foolish for letting some stranger make her question everything she's come to know about Bill. "I'm sorry. She really made it sound like there was a lot more between you, and all the things she said were things that have already gone through my mind. I guess hearing someone actually say them suddenly made it all very real.

"I know it has to be hard for anyone to take on someone else's children, and it made sense what she said about you being a bachelor and never having the responsibility of marriage, or even living with someone. It would be such a change to your lifestyle."

"Babe, I'm so ready for this change. I love being with you and the girls. I've wanted my own family for a long time. I've just never met anyone I wanted to share that with until you. I've dated a lot of women, but I haven't been in a relationship since high school--I told you that, and that was kid stuff, it wasn't real. Let me prove to you that this is right. It's what I want more than anything, but we've got to talk when there's a problem; you can't shut down on me."

She puts her head down on his shoulder and starts to cry. "I know. I'm sorry."

He brushes her hair. "Shhh, it's okay--please don't cry." In an effort to lighten the mood, he smiles. "I'll let you make it up to me." He leans down to kiss her. Cate looks up, laughs, and thinks, *Now his eyes are back to that beautiful bright blue. Oh, kissing him is so disarming. I just want to melt every time.*

He pulls her to her feet. "Come here. I want to dance with you again." Suddenly with a touch of a little clicker there's soft music playing throughout the whole apartment, just like magic. Then, before she knows what's happening, she's in his arms. He's holding her so tight she can barely breathe.

As they move slowly together to the soft music, all he can think is how much he wants her. He's going to do his best to make sure she wants him just as much and forgets about leaving tonight.

He starts kissing her very slowly, moving from her lips to her neck and back again. Cate's mind and body are turning to mush in his hands. She can't concentrate; she knows she should leave, but all she wants to do is stay. Her mind is racing in all directions at once. *Oh, his kisses are so incredible, no, no, no, not my neck. Oh, damn. I'm in trouble.*

Her brain is saying no, but the words can't make it to her lips and her body is screaming yes. She knows she should stop him, but she doesn't want to. They start moving toward his bedroom. She keeps telling herself she shouldn't do this, but her body is not getting the message from her brain.

In his bedroom, he continues to kiss her, rubbing his hands up and down her back. Gently he turns her around and starts ever so slowly unzipping her dress inch by inch, kissing every inch as the zipper lowers. This sends shivers up and down her spine. When her dress is completely unzipped, he gently turns her back around and starts kissing along the neckline of the dress. He slides the dress off of both shoulders at once and her dress pools around her feet. He takes a slight step back to get a better look. He lets out a low deep growl, and takes her hand so she can step out of the dress. He moves back to her neck and whispers, "Damn, you're beautiful."

Cate can't control her own reactions any longer, and her mind has trouble understanding what's happening, as she thinks, *What am I doing? My hands are unbuttoning his shirt. My body is in complete mutiny, it's totally ignoring my brain. Oh no! Protection, protection!*

She realizes she must have said that out loud, because he responds, "Don't worry, I've got it covered." She wonders if that was meant to be a pun? She finally surrenders and thinks, *This is it -- it's finally happening. His kisses and his touch are so soft and tender, I think I'm going to explode.*

CHAPTER 32

Cate wakes with a start, looks at the clock on the bedside table, and is shocked to see the time. She's panicked, "Oh God, oh God! It's 5 a.m. Oh damn, I've got to get back to Pat and Debbie's before everyone gets up."

He slowly opens those sexy eyes and says, "Okay, just one more minute," as he pulls her back down into his arms. "Cate, thank you for spending the night with me. I've wanted to make love to you since the first time I looked into those gorgeous big green eyes. I don't want to let you leave my bed, ever, and if it was for any reason other than Kaylee and Shawn, I wouldn't. So, as much as it kills me, I'll let you go for now."

She touches his face. "Believe me, I don't want to leave either. It would be so easy to stay here with you all day, but I've got to be back before everyone gets up."

He nods his head, "I know. Okay, let's go. I have some sweats you can wear if you want. They'll probably swallow you up, but I'm sure it will be more comfortable than getting back into that dress."

She looks around at their clothes scattered around the room. "No, I'd rather go home in my own clothes."

He warns her, "If you get back into that dress, I might have to get you out of it again."

She laughs. "Behave."

He reluctantly lets her go. "Hmmm, we'd better go while we can."

They arrive at the Wilsons' house by 5:57. Cate is thinking aloud that she should be able to sneak in and get into the shower before anyone gets up. Bill just looks at her and laughs. "I love you, Cate Wilson. You're so cute, thinking you have to sneak in like a school girl. You make me happy."

She leans over to kiss him goodbye. "I love you too, Bill Sullivan, and even though you're laughing at me, you make me happy, too."

He grabs her hand as she starts to get out of the car. "Whoa, you finally say 'YOU LOVE ME', then you want to jump out of the car?"

"Sorry, I gotta run."

"Can I call you later? Maybe we can have lunch with your mom so that Pat and Debbie can have a little more time with the girls?"

She looks back at him and wonders what she's done to deserve this wonderful man. She just smiles. "That would be really great. Call me."

She does her best to enter the house as quietly as possible. She laughs to herself, thinking, *I do feel like a teenager sneaking home before my parents wake up. I can't get this silly grin off my face. Last night, or I should say this morning, was incredible. I didn't realize how much I've missed sex. Bill is incredible, very incredible.*

Suddenly she's startled by her mother's voice. "Good morning, Catherine."

"Mom! What are you doing up this early?"

"What are you doing sneaking in this early?"

"Is everyone up?"

"No, you have time to go shower and dress before they wake up."

"Great. Would you fix some coffee while I shower?"

"Yep, get moving. I can't wait to hear about your evening."

Cate rushes in to shower and dress before Pat and Debbie get up. She hopes they don't realize that she didn't come home last night. Although it might be silly, she doesn't want them thinking badly of her.

Thirty minutes later, she walks back into the kitchen where her mom is waiting with two cups of coffee. Phoebe says, "I heard you coming, so I just poured us each a cup. Let's go on the patio so we can talk." Phoebe is dying to hear about Cate's evening, "So young lady, it must have been some evening for you to come in with the sun."

Cate smiles and can't believe how happy she feels. "It was a great evening, and yes, Bill won the award. We danced for hours--it was wonderful. The only glitch was one of his ex-girlfriends was there and tried to play head games with me. I almost let it work, but thankfully Bill insisted we talk things through and we worked it out."

Phoebe just raises her eyebrows. "Well, by the way you're glowing this morning I would say you did work it out. It makes me happy to see you so alive and smiling again."

Cate kisses her mom's cheek. "I am happy. I didn't think I would ever feel this way again. Mom, I'm falling in love with him."

"Oh, Cate, I'm so happy for you. I think Bill is a wonderful man, and I can see by the way he looks at you that he just adores you."

Cate can't seem to wipe the silly grin off her face. "Oh, by the way, Bill wants to take you and me to lunch today and give Pat and Debbie some quality time with the girls before we leave in the morning."

Phoebe continues to be impressed with how thoughtful Bill is. "Well, that'll be nice. Where are we going?"

Cate starts to get up as she hears Kaylee calling her in the kitchen, back to reality. "I'm not sure. He said he'd call later with the plans."

CHAPTER 33

At 11:30 another big black limo pulls up in front of the Wilsons'. Debbie catches a glimpse of it as she's passing through the living room to get Shawn's diaper bag for their tip to the Children's Museum. "Cate, Bill's here. My neighbors are going to think we won the lottery."

When Cate opens the door, Bill is standing there looking like a god. She feels the butterflies start to wake up in her stomach. "Wow, another limo."

He flashes that smile. "Nothing but the best for you two beautiful ladies."

Phoebe is just as anxious as Cate. She likes the idea of riding in a limo, but she suddenly feels that maybe she's underdressed, even though both Cate and Bill are wearing jeans. She turns to Bill and asks if she's dressed okay. He says, "Yes, you're fine. It's very casual. We're having lunch at a little restaurant on the lake. I just wanted to be able to give all of my attention to my two lovely dates. After all, it's not every day a man gets to escort two hot women at the same time."

Phoebe grabs her purse. "Well, I like it. It's not often I get to ride in style."

The ride to the restaurant is filled with light, easy conversation, and Phoebe really enjoys getting out of a limo and having people turn to see if it's someone famous. The restaurant is crowded, but Bill has a table reserved right next to the windows that overlook the lake. Cate tells her mother all about their lunch cruise around the lake the day before and asks Bill to fill Phoebe in on some of the history. He obliges and gives a brief history of some to the landmarks they can see from the window.

Phoebe is really enjoying herself; it's been a while since she's been out on the town. She thanks Bill again for including her in their plans. Cate's happy that her mom and Bill get along so well. She could never be with someone that Phoebe disapproved of.

They order coffee and dessert to finish off their meal. While they are waiting, Cate excuses herself, so she can call Debbie and check on the kids. Walking away, she can't help but think how much she loves seeing her mother smile. For a while she didn't know if either of them would ever smile again.

When Cate leaves, Bill leans in and lowers his voice. "Phoebe, while Cate's gone, I'd like to ask you something."

"Sure."

"I want to ask Cate to marry me, and I'd like to know if I have your blessing, and if you think it's too soon."

"Wow! I wasn't expecting that. Well, you do have my blessing. I think you've been great for her, and I think you're a good man, inside where it really counts. Now, is it too soon? Maybe, but sometimes you just know when you've met right person, and with all she and I have both been through, I know how short time can be, and I know you shouldn't waste a minute of happiness, because we never know how long we have."

"Do you think Cate will think it's too soon?"

"Probably, but she's still wrestling with feeling guilty about dating because it's only been a little over two years since Sean's death."

They stop their conversation, because Bill sees Cate heading back to the table. "Here she comes; please don't mention this to her."

"No worries."

Cate looks at them, knowing something is going on. "Hey, you two look pretty serious."

Bill covers. "No, I was just telling your mom a little about Sullivan Enterprises."

Phoebe goes along. "Yes, I am impressed by all of your accomplishments."

Before Cate can ask any more questions, Bill changes the subject. "While I have both of you together, I'd like to invite you to my 4th of July picnic at my house." Turning to Phoebe he explains, "My family takes turns hosting the holidays, and I, of course, wanted the ones that I could blow things up on. So, I do New Year's Eve and 4th of July. Mom, of course does Christmas, Cindy does Thanksgiving, and TJ gets Easter and Labor Day."

Cate is feeling a little more at ease with making plans with Bill for more than a couple of weeks in advance. Some of her fears are starting to subside, but she knows she still has a ways to go, so she defers to Phoebe. "Mom, what do you think?"

Phoebe of course is up for having fun after the past several months of hospitals and rehab. "I'm in, especially if there'lll be fireworks."

Bill laughs. "Oh, there will be lots of fireworks. The girls will love it--my niece and nephews will be there, and they can swim and run around; then we can sit back and watch the fireworks."

Phoebe says she would love to meet Bill's family and she reflects on how quickly the year is flying by. She can't believe that the 4th of July is only two months away.

CHAPTER 34

The first few days after the awards banquet are very trying for Cate, thanks to Hector and his wife, who lives for the gossip and society pages. Hector makes a point to be sure everyone at work knows Cate's seeing Bill.

She didn't even consider that their pictures would be in the papers in Charleston, and easily accessible on the internet. It was uncomfortable at first when everyone was asking questions, but Cate is also a little relieved, because now there's nothing to try to keep hidden.

After the first week, things die down and the talk of the office turns to something new. Everyone seems happy for Cate and Bill—everyone except Hector, who knew all along there had to be another reason for Bill to just come in and promote Cate so quickly.

Now Hector is sure that the only reason Bill made her the business manager is because he wanted to get into her pants. Of course, he doesn't come out and say what he's thinking, but he definitely gets in his digs when given the chance.

Over the next few weeks, Cate notices a difference in Hector's demeanor when she's around, and she's heard of some of the comments he's passed to other employees, but she tries to ignore it and hopes it will pass.

She doesn't mention anything to Bill, because she and Hector have never really seen eye-to-eye, but they've always been able to work together for the greater good of Sunrise Printing's best interests. She keeps telling herself at least he can't make her life miserable, since he's not her boss anymore.

Even dealing with Hector, Cate is happier in her job than she's ever been, and it's not just because she's dating the boss. She finally feels challenged and significant to the success of the business.

Every time Bill sends her a little instant message, she's still amazed that this feels so right to her. It's like everyone knowing freed her from a lot of guilt. Seems it's true that "the truth will set you free." Trying to keep things quiet made her feel like she was doing something wrong--and the sex, wow, making love with Bill is so amazing. He's so gentle and loving and strong, and thorough, very thorough. It's hard for her to keep from smiling whenever she thinks of him. Being in love is so exhilarating.

Bill, of course, couldn't be happier now that the cat's out of the bag, but he didn't care if everyone knew from the beginning. Seems like word has spread around the corporate office too, and Laura let's him know there are several broken-hearted ladies around the office, but he just laughs it off.

It's finally July 3rd and everyone is looking forward to the long weekend. By 4:00 the office is like a ghost town with just Cate, Hector, and Julie left in the office. They decide to call it a day and leave for the holiday.

The next morning, Phoebe pokes her head into Cate's room. "Good morning, sunshine. You're up early for a holiday morning."

Cate is busy going over her list of necessities for the girls to bring to Bill's for this legendary 4th of July celebration she's been hearing so much about. She makes sure to bring their bathing suits, toys, and a change of clothes for each of them, just in case.

"Good morning, Mom. Yeah, I couldn't sleep. I guess I'm excited, this will be our first full family get-together with Bill's family. I know you'll like his parents; they're really friendly, warm people."

"I'm sure I will. I've been looking forward to meeting everyone. I know the girls will have a blast with the other kids, too."

Cate tells her mom not to forget to bring her swimsuit, and Phoebe looks at her like she just landed from another planet.

"Oh, I'm not wearing a swimsuit in front of all those people. Are you crazy?"

"I thought you might want to get in the pool with the girls."

"No. I'll leave that to you."

"Okay, if you're sure."

"Oh, I'm sure. What time are we heading over there?"

"Bill said everyone starts getting there around 3:00, so I thought we would go for about 2:00 in case he needs help getting things ready."

Phoebe nods. "That will work out great. The girls can take a nap before we go, so they can last for the fireworks."

"Yes, they will definitely need a nap before we go. The fireworks won't start until about 8:00, or so, when it gets dark. I hear it's a really big to-do."

Phoebe walks over and hugs Cate. "Have I told you how much I love seeing you happy again?"

She hugs her mom back. "Yes, you tell me all the time. I like being happy again, and I've noticed Kaylee and Shawn are happier, too--they really like Bill. Speaking of them, I think I hear the munchkins waking up. After breakfast, I'll take them to the park for a little while, so they can run around and get worn out and take an early nap."

"Good idea. I may try to take one too, so I can last. I'm really looking forward to seeing this mansion you've told me so much about."

CHAPTER 35

They pull up in Bill's driveway a little before 2:00, and Cate enters the code into a little box and the big iron gates part silently. Phoebe is impressed already. "Wow, you have a gate code--did he give you a key to his house, too?"

Cate laughs. "No, I told him I wasn't ready for that.

As they make their way around the curve, the trees open to the most magnificent house Phoebe's ever seen in person. "Oh, Cate--this is beautiful."

"I know. Wait till you see the inside and the back-entertainment area. I can't call it a patio like Bill does. We have a patio--this is an entire entertainment area."

The girls like going to Bill's house too; although they're too young to appreciate the opulence, they like the pool. Kaylee asks, "Mommy, are we going to get to go in Bill's pool today?"

"Yes, and his niece and nephews will be here for you to play with, too."

She looks a little confused. "What are niece and nephews?"

"That means they are Bill's sister's and brother's children."

Satisfied with the answer, Kaylee just says, "Oh." She grabs Shawn's hand and tells her they are going to play with niece and nephews. Shawn just laughs. She loves her big sister, and if Kaylee is happy, Shawn is happy too.

When they pull up in front of the house, Bill is outside talking to some men by a truck. He quickly wraps up his conversation and comes over to help Cate and Phoebe. "Hey, I'm glad you came early so we could have some time before the whole tribe gets here." He gives all around kisses. "Phoebe, good to see you--come in and we'll give you the tour."

Phoebe gets out of the car and just stands there taking it all in. "Bill, your home is absolutely beautiful." Bill takes her hand and leads her inside. They take her through the first floor, then out onto the patio.

Everything is bustling out there with caterers prepping the food, people setting up tables and chairs and a couple of tents with face painting and games for the kids. Down by the lake they can see several men busy setting up the fireworks display.

Cate is stunned. "Wow this really is a big event, I thought it was just a family barbeque. How many people are you expecting?"

Bill laughs. "It is a family barbeque, but it's 4th of July, so we have to do it up big."

Cate's still looking around at everything, thinking, *This is crazy. I don't know if I'll ever get used to this.*

Phoebe is thoroughly impressed as she glances out toward the lake. "Bill, this is incredible. Cate tells me you spend most of your time out here on the patio when you're home, and I can see why. This view is fantastic."

"Thanks, yes, this is my favorite part of the house. Please make yourself at home. I showed you where everything is, so don't be shy."

Bill walks over and puts his arm around Cate. "Is everything okay?"

She looks around and says, "Yeah, everything's fine. I'm just surprised at all this. I thought you might need help getting everything ready, but it looks like you already have all the help you need."

He gives her a gentle little kiss and smiles at his good fortune. "I have this catered every year, so everyone can just relax and enjoy themselves and no one is stuck doing all the work."

They hear someone calling Bill's name from inside. Bill turns to Phoebe. "That sounds like Mom and Dad. They've been dying to meet you."

Ted and Marjorie walk onto the patio and Bill meets them and kisses his mom and hugs his dad. Marjorie rushes over to Cate and Phoebe and kisses Cate and gives Phoebe a big hug. "You must be Phoebe. I'm Marjorie and this is Ted, and these two little beauties must be Kaylee and Shawn." She bends down and gives them each a hug and a kiss on the head. "Phoebe, it's so nice to meet you, and Cate, your girls are beautiful--they look just like you."

Cate feels the tension melt away. She really likes being around Bill's family. They've made her feel welcome since the first time she met them. "Thanks! They're itching to get in the pool, but I told them they have to wait until the other children get here. I don't want them to burn out too quickly."

Marjorie turns to Bill. "How about some wine, so Phoebe and I can get the prime seats and get to know one another?"

"Yes ma'am, coming right up. Phoebe, do you want wine, or can I get you some iced tea?" Phoebe says she can only have one glass of wine and would rather save that for later in the evening, so she goes with iced tea for now.

Phoebe, Marjorie, and Ted get comfortable and quickly realize they have a lot in common, including knowing many of the same people. Before long the rest of his family arrives, and the party is in full swing.

Bill pulls away from the men, who are all giving their opinions on how the fireworks should be set up, and makes his way over to Cate at the pool with the girls. "Hey, are you doing okay?" He notices she wore a one-piece swimsuit, but even though she's not showing a lot of skin, it hugs her body perfectly.

Cate smiles up at him. "Yes. This is great. Your family is great. Looks like our moms have become fast friends, and the girls are having a blast. This is wonderful."

"Good. I love having you and the girls here, and if you like this, you'll love what happens after dark."

With an evil little grin, she replies, "I always love what happens after dark with you."

He raises his eyebrows and puts his hand to his chest. "Why, Ms. Wilson, you shock me."

"Good--you're not an easy man to shock."

Before they can go any further with the flirting, Kaylee interrupts. "Mommy, Mommy, Emma said I'm going to be her cousin, and you're going to be her new aunt. Is that true?"

She and Bill just look at one another and laugh. Cate's a little embarrassed, and clears her throat before answering, "Oh well, hum, I don't know. Why don't we just start with you two being really good friends, okay?"

Kaylee thinks for a second. "Okay, but I think I would like to be her cousin."

Cate glances at Bill again, trying hard not to laugh out loud, and turns back to Kaylee. "Okay, well, we'll have to see how things go."

Satisfied with that, Kaylee says, "Okay," and runs off with Emma, her new best friend.

She looks back at Bill, and he's grinning from ear to ear, "What are you smiling about?"

"Me? Nothing, just smiling."

She rolls her eyes. "Right. I'm going to take Shawn out of the water for a while and see if mom needs anything. Stop smiling."

He laughs and grabs Shawn, so she can dry off. Once she wraps a towel around herself and wraps Shawn up in another one, she makes her way toward the table were Phoebe and Marjorie are deep in conversation.

As she's approaching the table, she reflects on what Emma told Kaylee. *Her new aunt? Where would she get that from? But it's true that I have given way to fantasizing about what it would be like for us to be a family. I never want me or the girls to forget Sean, but Bill would be a great stepdad and husband, one day. Whoa, where did that come from? I can't believe I had that thought, but if we are going to be part of another family one day, this would be a great one.*

When Cate reaches the table, both ladies stop talking and Phoebe asks her if she needs a break from the little ones. Cate says she wants to go put some dry clothes on Shawn first and fix her a little bit to eat, and asks her mom if she needs anything.

Phoebe says no, she's fine and that she and Marjorie have quite a few mutual acquaintances. Marjorie and Ted went to the same high school as Phoebe, they were two years ahead of her, so, they never knew one another, but they knew a lot of the same people.

Cate is surprised. "Wow, really? Guess it really is a small world."

Marjorie pats Cate's hand. "Are you enjoying yourself, honey?"

"Definitely. Everything is great, and I love being around your family. You are all so close--reminds me of Mom and I."

"Good. We love having you here. Kaylee and Shawn are delightful; they are so well behaved."

"Thank you, and thank you for welcoming us to your family."

CHAPTER 36

As the sun starts to set, there's a buzz of anticipation as everyone starts thinking of the fireworks. Bill tells everyone that it will be about another thirty minutes and everyone starts making bathroom runs, getting drinks, and settling in for the show. Cate is sitting close to Bill, with Shawn playing on the ground right at her feet. She shakes her head and says, "This is crazy. I can't believe you hire a professional company to do your fireworks."

He gives her a quick kiss on the head. "If you're going to do it, do it right and leave the heavy lifting to the professionals. I usually go down and hit the button to get things started, but I'd rather be up here with you. If you could see the road from here, you'd see about a mile of cars that park out there every year to watch our display."

She's surprised. "Really? That's unbelievable."

He seems very proud of his fireworks display, and Cate is getting excited to see what the hype is all about. He turns to her again, with his eyes shining like a little boy's. "Wait till it starts--it's really great. Once it gets started, do you think you could get the girls settled with your mom and take a walk with me down to the gazebo?"

She's surprised that he would want to leave once the fireworks start, since that's all she's been hearing about for at least a month, and she wants to see the girls' faces.

"I kind of wanted to watch the fireworks with the girls--they've never seen a real fireworks display before."

He can't believe he didn't think of that. "We'll wait a few minutes before we go, and we'll be back before it's over, I promise. It lasts about forty-five minutes."

"Oh, wow, okay. I just have to make sure Mom's okay with it."

Once the fireworks start, the girls are mesmerized; they don't even notice Cate leave.

Bill and Cate walk down to the gazebo, which is halfway between the house and the lake where they are igniting the fireworks. They start off holding hands; then Bill puts his arm around her and pulls her closer. She thinks, *This is really nice*.

When they get to the gazebo, he pulls her closer and gives her the longest, deepest, most romantic kiss ever. As usual, she melts right into his amazing kisses. He whispers in her ear that he loves her and wants to hold her like this forever.

Meanwhile the fireworks are exploding above them in beautiful red, white, and blue colors. They stop kissing for a minute and look up just in time to see another amazing explosion. When she turns back to look in his eyes, she's stunned to see him down on one knee, holding a tiny baby-blue box in his hand.

Before the magnitude of what 's happening can register in Cate's brain he says, "Cate, I fell in love with you the very first time I saw you, and every day I know you, I love you more. I want to marry you and raise Kaylee and Shawn with you. Will you be my wife?"

Cate is in shock. All she can do is stare at him with her hands to her mouth. She can't even form words. Finally, he says, "Well, what do you say?"

She feels the tears streaming down her face as she nods her head and barely manages to get the word "YES" out of her mouth. She can actually see the relief wash over his face, and he breaks into the biggest smile. He slips the ring on her finger and stands up. He says he loves her over and over as he kisses away her tears.

"I love you, Cate. I've waited for you my whole life. I promise I will make you happy, and these are the only kind of tears I ever want to see you cry again. Happy tears are good, right?"

She is still having trouble forming words. "Yes, they're good. I wasn't expecting this at all. I couldn't even speak."

"I noticed. I started to get worried you would say no. That's why I wanted to do this in private. I didn't want you to feel pressured to say yes, and I didn't want everyone to see me crushed if you said no."

She laughs. "You're so funny. I love you. I never thought I would love again, then God sent you into my life and gave me a second chance at happiness."

He looks up at another explosion. "Let's get back up to the house for the finale; then we can share the news with everyone."

She grabs his hand. "Did anyone know you were going to do this?"

He looks down sheepishly. "Only everyone."

As he pulls her along toward the house, she can't believe it. "What? Did my mom know?"

"Yep. I asked her approval weeks ago."

"No way. I can't believe she kept this a secret."

"What can I say? She loves me too."

All she can do is shake her head. "Yes, she really does."

As they walk back up to the house, everyone is looking at them instead of the fireworks. Bill smiles and holds up her hand. Everyone starts screaming and clapping. Both their mothers are on their feet and hugging each other. The kids are all a little confused about what's going on and wondering what they missed. When the fireworks end, they all go inside so everyone can get a better look at the ring.

When Cate sees it for the first time in the bright lights of the kitchen, she's struck by how beautiful it is. It's a gorgeous square-cut diamond, the biggest she's ever seen, with three emerald baguettes going down each side. Cate is stunned. She thinks, *Oh my God, I don't know what this thing cost, but I know it had to be a lot. I can't wear this every day. What if something happens to it?*

The women are all gushing over the ring and hugging her. Then Cindy asks Bill what the total weight is. Cate is floored when he says three carats, platinum setting. Cate looks down at her hand again. *Oh, holy hell--this ring is worth more than everything I own.*

He must have seen the look on her face, because he comes over, kisses her and says, "Don't worry, it's insured." She just shakes her head again in disbelief, thinking, *This man is amazing. I think he really does read my mind.*

CHAPTER 37

It's after midnight when everything winds down and everyone starts going home. Bill whispers in her ear that he wants her to stay the night. He says his parents offered to take her mom home, and the girls are already sleeping on the floor in the den, and they can sleep on the couches in the den with the girls.

Cate talks to her mom and she's okay with it, so Cate agrees to stay. She's glad she brought an extra outfit for the girls; unfortunately, she didn't think to bring one for herself.

Once everyone leaves, Cate starts to straighten the kitchen, but Bill takes her hand and leads her to his bedroom. He starts kissing her and unbuttoning her shirt, but she stops him. "We can't -- the girls are in the den."

He keeps kissing her. "They're sleeping."

She takes a step back from him. "I know, but what if they wake up?"

Bill grabs her hand and kisses her fingertips. "You know, once we're married, we're going to make love when they're in the house asleep."

As much as she hates it, she takes her hand back. "I know, but that's once we're married."

He takes a step back, looks in her eyes and realizes it's not happening tonight; he lets out a low, deep sexy growl, and says, "You're killing me, woman. Do you know how much I want you right now?"

Cate wants him just as much as he wants her, but she just doesn't feel right about it with the girls in the house. Bill gives her a quick kiss, then walks over to his dresser and pulls out a couple pairs of sweat pants and tee shirts. He tosses a set to Cate and tells her to get comfortable and they'll go snuggle on the couch and admire that ring.

She takes his hand and kisses his palm. "Thanks for understanding-- and I've been wanting to just stare at this thing all night."

After changing their clothes, they lie down together on one of his big leather couches in the den with the girls bedded down on the floor looking like two little angels. Cate can't get over how right and wonderful this feels, the four of them in this big cozy room like a real family.

Bill lies there holding her in his arms, as she's holding her hand out looking at the ring. He asks, "What are you thinking?"

She smiles. "Oh, just admiring my ring and thinking how lucky I am."

He pulls her a little closer. "I'm the one that's lucky--I'm a very blessed man. I've been very successful in business. I've put in a lot of hard work to build my business, but I always knew I wanted someone to share it all with. I kind of started thinking maybe that wasn't meant to be. Then one magical day there she was, the most beautiful woman I've ever laid eyes on, huddled with two little angels under a shelter in a storm."

She sits bolt upright. "Wait. What?"

He looks up at her, smiling. "What's wrong? Don't you remember meeting me that stormy day when my car broke down right in front of that dentist's office where you were taking shelter?"

She blinks, trying to comprehend what he's saying. "Of course, I remember, but I didn't think you remembered me."

He laughs. "Didn't remember? You've been all I could think about from that moment on."

She grabs her head. "Oh my God! I didn't think you... I mean you never said anything."

"Neither did you."

She can't believe after all this time he never even mentioned that he remembered that day. "I didn't think you remembered me, and after the way I treated you, I was hoping you didn't. When you walked into the conference room with Mr. Lawden and announced you bought Sunrise, I almost fainted. All I could think was *Great, now I'm fired*, and I prayed you didn't remember me. When you kept looking at me, I just knew it was over."

Now he's really laughing. "Is that why you were so quiet and didn't ask any questions?"

"Yes--I couldn't speak, I could barely breathe, and you kept staring at me with those eyes. I wanted to crawl under the table."

"You silly girl. I couldn't stop looking at you. You were even more beautiful than I remembered."

"I couldn't believe of all the people in the world to buy Sunrise, it would be you. I mean, what are the chances?"

He knows it's time to come clean. "It wasn't by chance."

Cate furrows her brow, confused. "What do you mean?"

"I guess I can tell you now, since you've already agreed to marry me. You're the reason I bought Sunrise."

She almost falls off the couch. "What!?"

"Well, you're the reason I checked into Sunrise. Once I did some analysis and thought about how much we could save enterprise wide on printing and graphics, it made perfect sense."

"But how did you know I worked there?"

"I did a little research."

"You checked me out? What, like a background check? You didn't even know my name."

"You told me your name was Cate."

"And you found out where I worked just from my first name?"

"Well, not me personally, but I've got people."

"People? You mean like a detective? Wait, did you have Johnny check me out?"

"Kind of. Are you upset?"

"I don't know, maybe. I mean, what else did you find out about me?"

"Just the most important things. Your name, where you worked, if you were single. Cate, I had just met the woman I wanted to marry. I wasn't leaving things to chance and hope I'd run into you again."

"Wow. I don't know whether to be mad or flattered. Why didn't you say something sooner?"

He holds up two fingers. "Couple of reasons. First, I wasn't 100% sure you remembered me. Second, I didn't want you to think I was a stalker and scare you off."

"Well, I probably would have thought you were a stalker, but I can't believe you'd buy a company just to meet me."

"I wouldn't have bought it if I didn't think it was a sound business investment. I would have found another way to meet you. You're not really upset, are you?"

"I'm stunned. I just can't imagine someone going through all that trouble just to meet me."

He pulls her back down into his arms, "Cate, you're my dream come true, I'd do anything for you."

She settles back in next to him, they fit perfectly together. She just stares, studying his handsome face and tries to make sense of someone buying a company just to meet her.

One of the things he loves most about her, is her inability to understand just how beautiful she is and the effect she has on men.

CHAPTER 38

The next morning, he wakes her up with kisses. "Good morning, sleepy head."

She moans and turns over, when she opens her eyes, she sees the empty pillows and blankets on the floor. She jolts awake. "Oh, where are the girls?"

He eases her back down. "Relax. They're in the kitchen; we cooked breakfast."

She opens her eyes wide. "You and the girls?"

He stands up and offers his hand to help her up. "Yep, we made pancakes, and they're waiting to serve you."

They walk hand-in-hand to the kitchen, where it looks like a storm blew through. "Wow, look at this. Did you two help Bill make pancakes?"

Both girls are all smiles and Kaylee answers for both, as usual. "Yeah Mommy, it was fun. Bill let us mix it all up. We spilled a little, but Bill said it was okay."

Cate kisses the girls thinking, *Spilled a little? The kitchen looks like the flour exploded in here, but they all look so proud.* She looks at those two precious, proud faces. "Sure, it's okay, and we'll get it cleaned up later. I can't wait to taste your pancakes."

They all sit at the table and Bill serves their plates. The pancakes are surprisingly good; breakfast is wonderful. The girls are so happy as they tell her how they made the pancakes. Cate doesn't care how much mess they made--it's worth it to see them this happy.

As they finish their breakfast, Bill asks what she would think about the three of them spending the rest of the weekend at his house. Cate looks from him to the girls. "I don't know. I don't have clothes for me, or them, and I really have to check on my mom."

Bill, always one with a solution says, "No problem. After breakfast, we'll all get cleaned up and go to your house. We'll get some clothes and toys, and we can even bring Phoebe back to spend the weekend with us if you want."

At this, Kaylee adds her two cents. "Yeah, Mommy--can we, please? I want to go swimming again."

And Shawn just repeats everything her big sister says. "Yeah, go swimming."

Cate looks around and sees three faces with the same expectant look. How can she say no? Especially when she loves the idea of being with him for the whole weekend. "Okay."

Kaylee yells, "Yay! Thank you, Mommy."

Bill leans over and whispers in her ear, "Yes, thank you, Mommy," and kisses her cheek.

She takes another look around the kitchen, and adds, "Okay, but we have to clean up this mess first, and we still have the mess outside to clean up from last night."

Bill picks up their plates and takes them to the sink. "Don't worry about that. Trudy will be here to take care of it."

Cate looks confused. "Who's Trudy?"

"Trudy, my housekeeper."

Cate acts like she's never heard the word before. "Housekeeper?"

He can't help but laugh at the look on her face. "Yeah, you don't think I keep this place looking like this on my own, do you?"

"I guess I never really thought about it."

As he starts putting dishes and pans in the sink, he explains, "Trudy's been my housekeeper for the last five years, since I built this place. She comes in once a week and whenever I have parties. Today she'll have her husband and son with her to clean up outside; they take care of the grounds and the pool."

Cate looks around again. "Oh...well, I have to at least clean up all this flour and our dishes."

"What are you talking about? I just said Trudy would be here soon to clean up."

"I know, but I can't have her thinking you've hooked up with some slob--and don't shake your head at me."

He does shake his head as he walks out of the kitchen. "You're so adorable; I love you. I'm going to take a quick shower, so please don't go overboard. Trudy will be pissed if she doesn't have something to clean."

When he leaves, she glances around again thinking, *Housekeepers, groundskeepers, professional fireworks. I don't know about all of this. I guess we both have major lifestyle changes to adjust to.*

After getting the kitchen at least presentable enough so Cate feels that Bill's housekeeper won't run out screaming, they head over to her house to get clothes for the weekend. Once the girls are all cleaned and changed and have gathered a ton of toys to take back to Bill's, he suggests they bring some extra clothes to leave at his house.

Cate feels kind of weird about that but realizes he's right--now that they're engaged, they'll probably be spending more time at his place. So, she brings them each some pj's and a couple sets of clothes.

Bill asks Phoebe if she wants to come back and spend the rest of the weekend with them, but she says no. She has plans with some friends she used to work with. They're picking her up later for dinner and a movie.

When they get back to Bill's house, everything is spotless, and Trudy is busy cleaning the patio. Bill introduces Trudy to Cate and the girls. Trudy is about forty-five, short, with short brown hair and a friendly smile. Bill tells her they're engaged and shows her the ring; she squeals with happiness and kisses them both. Cate's relieved that it seems like she's truly happy for them.

When she found out about Trudy, she was concerned that Trudy would think, *Great, now I have to clean up after them, too,* but she genuinely seems happy for Bill.

She calls him Mr. Bill--Cate thinks that's cute. Trudy calls her husband, Sam, and their sixteen-year-old son, Morgan over to meet Cate. Sam is the grounds and pool guy and Morgan helps his dad on weekends. Bill explains that they take care of his parents' and his sister's houses, too.

Trudy fixes them salads for lunch and grilled cheese sandwiches for the girls. After lunch, they go relax in the den and put a movie on while the girls play on the floor with their toys.

Cate thinks how nice it is, just like a real family. She never really got to have this with Sean; he was gone more than he was home, and then he was just gone.

As the movie is ending, the girls are starting to get restless and bored with their toys, so they all suit up and hit the pool. After a couple of hours in the pool, the girls are winding down, so they give them a snack and settle them down with pillows and blankets on the floor of the den again and put on a Disney movie, and they're out in no time. Bill and Cate finally get a little quiet time to snuggle and talk.

Bill nuzzles her ear. "Hmmm, I love this day."

She cuddles in a little closer. "Me too. I'm glad you suggested we stay."

He glances down at Kaylee and Shawn curled up among the pillows, blankets, and toys on the floor, then back at Cate and tells her, "You know, y'all could just move in permanently."

She gives him a quick little kiss and says, "We will, once we're married."

This sparks a twinkle in his eyes. "Speaking of which, let's set a date."

She looks at him like he just grew a third eye. "You want to set a date already? We're barely engaged."

Instead of being discouraged, this eggs him on. "Yep, and I actually have a date in mind."

Now she knows he must have had too much sun. "Really? And when is that?"

"October 17th."

"What? This October? That's only three months away. Why October 17th?"

"That will be exactly one year since we met under the shelter that stormy day, and it's a Saturday this year, so it will work out great."

She blinks, thinking this will help her understand better what he's saying. Surely, she must have misheard him. "But that's only three months away."

Now he's smiling that sexy, naughty smile of his. "I know. It'll be hard to wait that long."

She thinks she's starting to hyperventilate. "Long? How am I going to plan a wedding in three months?"

"We'll get Laura to help--and Cindy, Sherrie, and both our moms will be glad to help too."

He obviously is not hearing her. "But Bill, that's only three months away."

He shakes his head. "Three months--got it. That's plenty of time. It can be as big or small as you want. Hell, we can elope if you want. I don't care; I just want you to be my wife."

She turns to logic. "Sure, October will be a year from the first time we met, but we've really only known each other for about seven months. I mean, we haven't even seen each other's bad sides yet. We haven't even had a real fight yet."

"Do you want to have a fight?"

"No. Of course not, but what if we rush into this then realize we can't live together? When I get married again I want it to be for the rest of my life."

"I know, I do too. That's why I've waited so long. Cate, I know we haven't known each other that long, but I know I love you and you're the woman I want to spend the rest of my life with. I've known people that dated for years and had their marriages fail, and I've known people that got married after dating for a month that are still together ten years later. I know we're right, and you do too. Don't be afraid."

She sits back against the couch and tries to think of something else to say. She's not sure if his argument makes sense, or if she thinks he's lost his mind.

The remainder of the weekend is spent just enjoying their time as a family. Cate is constantly impressed with how good Bill is with the girls. Cate feels a little sad when it's time to leave Sunday evening to go home, but can't wait to see Phoebe and tell her about Bill's suggestion for a wedding date.

CHAPTER 39

Monday morning comes all too soon. As Cate drives to work, she reflects on the best weekend she's had in years she thinks, *It's been some weekend--I went from dating a fantastic guy on Thursday when I left work to being engaged and asked to plan a wedding in three months. THREE MONTHS! Bill says it's doable, and it probably is, but it's a lot more than just the wedding. We'll be moving into his house and I don't even know what school district he's in, and what about Mom? She says she'll be fine, but I hate the thought of leaving her alone.*

Her mind has been going non-stop since Bill brought up the idea of an October wedding. Before she realizes it, she's pulling into her parking spot at work.

She gets settled in with her cup of coffee and starts to scroll through her email, but she's finding it hard to get her mind off the thought of possibly being married in three months. She shakes her head and says aloud, "Oh, good grief, I have to focus on work."

Julie happens to be passing her office and hears Cate talking. She glances at her desk phone and sees there are no lines lit. She walks over to the office door and sticks her head in, "Hey, Cate--you okay? Are you talking to yourself in here?"

A little embarrassed, Cate looks up. "Oh, Julie--yes, I guess I am. I didn't realize I was speaking out loud."

Julie's eyes just about pop out of her head when she spots the ring. "Oh, my God! Cate! Are you and Bill engaged? Look at that ring."

Cate glances down quickly and can't keep from smiling. "Yes, he proposed Friday night during the fireworks."

Julie rushes in and grabs Cate's hand, admiring the ring. "Oh, that's so romantic--congratulations."

Cate looks at the ring, admiring it too. "Thanks, but don't mention it to anyone else yet. I'm still trying to get used to it myself."

Julie laughs. "I won't have to tell anyone; they'll be able to see that ring from a mile away."

Cate furrows her brow. "You're right. Maybe I shouldn't wear it here. But it is beautiful, isn't it?"

Julie looks at Cate over her glasses. "Are you crazy? If a man gave me a ring like that, I'd never take it off. I'm so happy for you. Have you talked about a date yet?"

"We're thinking of one, but it's not decided yet."

Hector appears at Cate's door for their regular Monday morning briefing. "Date for what?"

When she sees him, she quickly puts her hand down on her lap and tries to change the conversation. "Oh, hi, Hector--how are we coming on the Handy Dan's order? Is it time to kick off the second billing yet?"

Julie excuses herself, looks back, and winks at Cate. Hector steps inside the office and sits in the chair across the desk from her. "Yeah, that's what I was coming to tell you."

As Cate starts to shuffle some papers on her desk, Hector catches a glimpse of the ring. "Wow! What's that on your hand?"

She should have known his eagle eye wouldn't miss a thing. "It's a ring."

He stands up to get a better look. "I can see that. That's some ring, did Bill give that to you?"

Cate reminds herself to take a deep breath before answering. "Yes, he proposed to me this weekend."

Hector's eyebrows shoot up in surprise. He didn't think Bill would be serious about someone like Cate. After all she's not exactly in Bill's class of people. Sure, she's beautiful, but he thought Bill was just having fun. "Proposed? Well, you're not wasting any time, are you?"

Cate's not sure what Hector is insinuating, but she doesn't like where this is going. "What do you mean?"

He throws his hands up. "Well that's what you women do, right? Y'all get the chance to date a rich guy, and you hook him as soon as you can."

She's quickly going from offended to pissed. "I can't speak for all women, Hector, but that has certainly never been my intention."

He just gives a little sarcastic laugh. "Well, intentional or not, you got him to give you the ring, didn't you?" He shakes his head as he turns to go out the door. "I gotta go check on my guys. I'll bring back the paperwork on Handy Dan's."

Cate is stunned and mad and talking to herself again. "Great. I sure didn't need him finding out about this first thing this morning. Ugh!"

Julie overheard the entire conversation, so she peeks her head back in and tries to comfort Cate. "Don't worry about him; he's not your boss anymore. In fact, you're marrying the boss, so he's the one that should be worried."

Cate tries to calm herself down. "Julie, you know I'm not like that. Hector's a jerk, yes, but he's good at what he does. I just don't want him starting the rumor mill going again."

Julie reaches over and takes Cate's coffee cup to go refill it for her and says, "I know you don't like people talking and that you're a private person, but everyone here knows the two of you, and they all know that Hector's been jealous of you since Bill took over and made you the Business Manager. Besides, just like when everyone found out you and Bill were dating, it will be big news today, but by tomorrow it will be business as usual."

Cate lets out a sigh. "Hmmm, I hope so."

Cate is glad when five o'clock finally arrives. She's exhausted and can't wait to get home. Once Hector set things off this morning, it seemed to all go downhill.

He, of course, couldn't wait to "happen" to mention to everyone that she and Bill are now engaged and his thoughts on the subject. This is not how she expected things to go. She's not sure what she expected, but it wasn't to be left feeling like she should be embarrassed, or that she has to defend herself against anyone thinking she's latched on to Bill for his money.

By the time she gets home with the girls, she's fit to be tied. Phoebe takes one glance at her and knows something's wrong. She asks, "Honey, why the long face? Bad day?"

Cate shakes her head yes and feels like she's on the verge of tears and answers, "Kind of, let me get the girls settled and I'll tell you about it while we get dinner ready."

Phoebe takes Shawn from her and starts to walk toward the bathroom to get her cleaned up for dinner. "Okay, I have a roast in the oven, so we just have to fix the salads and sides."

Cate smiles and feels a sense of relief wash over her. "Thanks, Mom. It's so nice to come home and not have to think of what to cook." She helps Kaylee get some toys out to keep them occupied until it's time to eat.

Cate gets back to the kitchen first and peeks in the oven; the roast smells wonderful. Before starting on the salad, she pours herself a glass of wine and takes a long, soothing swallow. Setting her glass down, she turns to see Phoebe entering the room. "Mom, do you think Bill and I are moving too fast with all of this?"

Phoebe looks at the now half-empty glass of wine and smiles. "Cate, you asked me that yesterday and my answer's still the same. I know you two are happy together, and I really believe you belong together. So why wait? You've got to stop worrying about what others think. Do what's right for you and your girls. The hell with everyone else. So, who's got you feeling like this?"

Cate glances down at her hand. "Hector. He saw my ring first thing this morning and insinuated that I got my hooks into a rich man and couldn't wait to reel him in."

"Hector? I should have known. You can't pay attention to what someone like him says. He's a sexist pig that thinks women should be barefoot and pregnant, waiting on their man hand and foot."

"I know you're right, but I'd just hate for anyone to think I've gotten where I am by using people."

"Cate, how many times have I told you, people will think what they want to think? You and Bill and the people that matter all know the truth. Don't deny yourself much deserved happiness because of small-minded people."

"Mom, I love you. You're always the voice of reason. So, tell me the truth--do YOU think getting married in October is just crazy soon?"

Phoebe takes Cate's hands in hers. "No, I don't. If you two wanted to get married tomorrow, I'd be on board. I see the way you look at each other, like you're the only two people in the world. Don't put off your happiness for a presumed protocol."

Cate kisses her mother's cheek. "But what about you?"

Phoebe looks a little confused. "What about me?"

"Well, if the girls and I move out, you'll be all alone."

"It's not like you're moving across the country. You'd only be going across town, and Dr. Donaldson said he thinks I can start driving again soon, so I'll be fine. I'm a big girl."

"I know, but I worry about you, especially since the stroke. What if something happens, and you're here all alone?"

"Honey, you worry too much about what ifs. I'll get me one of those button things you wear and press if you need help. I'll be fine."

Cate suddenly gets a great idea. "Hey, what if you come live with us? I mean, that house is big enough for three families. Oh, that would be great."

"Whoa, Cate, slow down. I'm not moving in with you and Bill. You two will just be starting your lives together as a family. That will be a big enough adjustment for the two of you without having a mother-in-law underfoot. You two will need your privacy, and I like having my own home. It will all work out. Now let's focus on the important stuff, like planning a wedding."

CHAPTER 40

Thanks to her mother, Cate is feeling much better by the time Bill calls. This is the first time she's talked to him all day; he was tied up in meetings and she was actually glad he couldn't call earlier, with the mood she was in.

It's almost 10:00, and he's just getting in. He's tired, too, and the sound of her voice gives him a feeling of peace. "Hi, beautiful, how was your day?"

Hearing him on the other end of the phone wakes up the little butterflies in her stomach. "Hey, handsome--better now."

He sits back to relax in his chair. "I miss you. I don't know if I'll be able to keep working in Charlotte all week and only seeing you on weekends. We'll have to figure something out."

She's a little surprised and not sure what this might mean. "I guess we'll have to give that some thought. Do you think we'll have to move to Charlotte?"

"That's a thought. Maybe I'll relocate our headquarters to Charleston, but we don't have to figure that out right now. Let's talk about our wedding. Have you decided if October 17th will be our date?"

"Well, we may be able to work it out. I've been thinking and I'm not sure how you feel about it, but I really don't want anything big, just family and a few close friends."

"I would love to invite the whole world to witness me marrying the most beautiful woman in the world, but if you want to keep it small, or if you want to elope, I don't care, as long as you marry me. I love you, girl."

"I love you, too. I was talking to Mom earlier and I'm a little worried about leaving her alone. Since her stroke, I worry about her all the time. That stroke happened so quickly--one minute she was fine, and the next she wasn't."

"I know you worry about her; maybe she can come live with us. There's plenty of room."

"I kind of suggested that to her, but she wouldn't hear of it. Said we needed our privacy and she did too."

Bill immediately says, "Okay, what about this? The basement already has a bedroom and a full bath--we add a kitchen and a separate entrance, then it's two separate living spaces, but she's still right there with us."

"Really?" Cate never even thought about that sort of compromise.

"Sure. I'll get my contractor to come out this weekend to work up some plans."

She realizes that this is one of the many reasons he is so easy to fall in love with. "Oh, Bill--that would be great, but before we go too far, I'll have to get her to agree to it."

"Let's get the plans drawn up first so she can see it laid out. Maybe she'll be more agreeable to it once she sees it on paper."

"You truly are the most wonderful man in the world."

"Yeah, well--it's easy when you're in love. Speaking of, did anyone notice your ring?"

"Oh yes, everyone." She hesitates for a moment to decide if she wants to tell him the whole story, but remembers what he said last time, they have to be able to talk about everything, so she goes with it.

"I was a little upset earlier, but I'm okay now."

"Upset--why?"

"Oh, just a comment Hector made, but he doesn't matter."

He sits up a little straighter. "What kind of comment?"

"Nothing really. It doesn't matter."

Bill knows it wasn't nothing, because Cate doesn't get upset over nothing. "I want to know what he said to upset you."

Feeling a little sorry she mentioned it, she knows it's too late now. "He just sort of insinuated that I didn't waste any time hooking you into marrying me. It did upset me a little, but after talking to my mom, she's right, he doesn't matter. All that matters is how we feel about each other."

Bill knows there has been tension between Cate and Hector for a long time, and he also knows Hector didn't like the idea of Cate being made a manager just like him, but so far, they have been working well together. "I'll have a talk with him."

"No! No. I don't want you to do that. Please."

"Cate, I'm not going to let some small-minded jerk that works for ME say stupid, hurtful things to you, and not do something about it."

Now she is sorry she brought it up. "Bill, please don't. I'm a big girl, I can handle it. I have to work with this guy every day and I can't have you making me look like I need you to fight my battles. I would lose everyone's respect, including my own."

He rubs his hand across his forehead in frustration. "Cate, I'm not going to sit back and let anyone insult you and do nothing."

"Bill, please. This is my job, my issue. I've worked with Hector for seven years now; he's just a jerk sometimes. At least he's not my boss anymore and I can deal with him.

I need to be able to tell you things without you thinking you have to rescue me, or fix it. I love that you want to, but you've got to let me handle my own problems. If things get too bad, I'll gladly let you sweep in and save me. Okay?"

"Cate, you've had enough hurt and sorrow in your life and I want nothing but happiness for you from now on. I can squash him like a bug, if you let me."

She laughs. "As tempting as that is--no. Thank you for wanting to be my hero, but a competent, strong business-woman like myself can handle her own problems."

He concedes, "You are a competent, strong, business-woman, and I know you can handle your own problems. I will respect your wishes, but I don't like it."

"Thank you. Now let's talk about something more fun. Do you have any special plans for this coming weekend?"

"No. I'm planning to leave Charlotte around lunch time Friday, so I can be home when you get off. Do you have something special you'd like to do?"

"Actually, I was wondering if you would mind going with me to look at new cars. I think I can now afford to replace my old clunker thanks to the big raise my boss gave me. I finally feel like I can breathe again." Suddenly she wonders if there is a sliver of truth to what Hector implied. "I hope you didn't promote me and give me that raise just because you were attracted to me."

"No, I didn't. I checked out everyone's work history, just like I do for all my businesses and made the decisions I felt were fair. I'm glad it's been good for you, and I would love to go with you to get a new car. If you tell me what you want, I'll make some calls."

Relieved by his answer, she gets back on track. "That would be great--I think I want an SUV. I always seem to have so much stuff to haul around for the girls. I think an SUV would be good, but not a real big one. I don't want to feel like I'm driving a bus."

"I think that's a good choice. Do you know what brand you like?"

"Not really; I don't know much about them. I thought I'd do a little research before Friday."

"Okay, just make sure you look for ones with the highest safety ratings. I want my girls to be safe."

"Will do. I love you."

"Love you too, babe."

When they hang up, she's feeling better and relieved that she did tell him about Hector--although for a minute she wasn't sure it was the right call.

Bill, on the other hand, is furious about the Hector situation. He decides he'll get with HR tomorrow and just make sure all his ducks are in a row in case he has to fire him.

CHAPTER 41

Cate is glad when Friday evening arrives. She reflects back on the week as she organizes her desk for Monday morning and thinks, *It's been a long week. Bill's right; it's getting tougher to go the whole week without seeing him.*

Even though they sometimes talk a couple of times a day and every night before they go to sleep, it's not like being able to hold and kiss each other and just relax together at the end of the day. She shakes her head and laughs to herself. *Listen to me. I can't believe I feel this way. I never thought I would again, especially not in such a short amount of time.*

She gathers up her stuff and can't wait to surprise him with the news that she can spend the whole weekend with him, alone. It's wonderful doing things as a family, but it's nice to have some adult time, too.

She admits she was excited when Debbie called to ask if she and Pat could come spend the weekend with the girls. They've been so great about everything. When she told them about the engagement, they were happy for her. She understands they have mixed emotions about things, but they've been nothing but supportive. They are such good people; she loves them, and she's happy Bill understands how important they are to her and the girls. She reminds herself of what an incredible man he is to be willing to basically take on two sets of in-laws.

She calls him when she gets home, to discuss their evening plans and surprises him with the news that she's free to spend the whole weekend with him.

She explains that Pat and Debbie came in to spend the weekend with the girls, and when she told them she was meeting him to go car shopping, they suggested she spend the weekend with him, so they wouldn't have to share the kids, and her mom practically pushed her out the door, saying they needed some private time together.

Bill is surprised and thrilled. "Wow! I owe them. I mean, I love the girls and love having them with us, but to have you all to myself for a whole weekend...I'm having all sorts of ideas, and they all involve having you naked."

She laughs. "Ooooh, that sounds promising, but we have to car shop first."

"If you wanted me to concentrate on cars, you shouldn't have led with the news that I get to keep you all weekend."

"Well, that will give you something to look forward to."

"Ugh, okay. Did you narrow down your choices?"

"Yes, but the SUV's rated highest for safety are also the most expensive. So, I think I may go with the Ford, or maybe the Hyundai. It's got the best warranty, and they both have pretty good safety ratings and are more in by budget."

He doesn't like either of those choices. "I've done a little research too--hope you don't mind. I would suggest the Volvo, Audi, or maybe a Mercedes."

She thinks he's lost his mind; after all, he does know how much she makes. She reminds him that those choices are out of her budget, but this doesn't sway him--he suggests she let him help out.

This is not where she intended things to go. She can't have him thinking she asked him to go with her to pick a car, so he would pay for it. She has to set this straight. "NO! That's not why I asked you to go with me."

He gives himself a mental slap; he should have known better. "I know that, and I didn't even think that for a minute. I just want you and the girls to have the best and be as safe as possible. Cate, we're going to be married in a few months, so either we can get the right car now, or I'll get you another one after we're married anyway."

She gets a little defensive. "You'll get me another one? What does that mean--I won't have a choice, and you'll be making all the decisions? I can buy my own car."

"Whoa, look--that is not what I meant. I'm sorry. I got a little carried away, and you will always have a choice; we're partners. Look, we have a whole weekend to ourselves. How about you come over; we'll get something to eat and start this conversation all over again."

Cate calms down immediately; she realizes Bill's not the type of guy who wants to control everything, so she agrees and tells him she'll be over soon. When they hang up Bill reminds himself that Cate is a very proud woman, and this is one of the things that he loves about her. He decides he'll just back off, make a few suggestions, and try not to push.

When Bill opens the door to let Cate in, he's pleasantly surprised at the beautiful sight before his eyes. Cate has on a sleeveless mint-green top with white jeans that fit just right and some cute little strappy sandals. All he can say is "Wow." She laughs and walks in and kisses him. He grabs her in his arms, pulls her closer, and gives her a deep sexy kiss. She feels herself melting into him; she loves that feeling.

He slowly pulls away, rubs his thumb down her cheek, and looks deep into her eyes and tells her he's sorry for upsetting her earlier. She smiles and says she's sorry too. They kiss again and Bill whispers in her ear that if she's hungry they'd better stop, or dinner will have to wait until later. She puts her hand on his chest, pushes him back a little, and says she is very hungry.

He grunts in disappointment; this make her laugh again.

They decide to drive into town and have an evening out. Eventually they get back to the subject of car shopping. He treads lightly when he suggests that she pay what her budget allows, and he will pay the rest. He lets her know he realizes she's proud and wants to do everything herself, but reminds her she's not alone anymore, that they're a team.

This time, she acknowledges she knows what he's saying, but she just doesn't feel right about it. She says maybe they should wait another couple of months and just buy it after they're married. He hears the disappointment in her voice and knows she had her mind set on finding something this weekend. He concedes and asks if she would agree to at least look at his choices and if she'd still rather go with one of her picks, he won't bug her about it anymore.

She agrees and asks if they can go first thing in the morning to look around. He raises his eyebrows at her and says, "Watch this." He takes out his phone and makes a call to someone named Kevin, gives him the makes and models of the cars she wants to see, and tells him to bring them for 9 a.m.

Cate looks confused and asks what that was about. He explains that Kevin is the broker he uses when buying cars and he will bring one of each to his house at 9 a.m. for her to test drive. Once she decides which one she wants, all she has to do is let Kevin know what color, and he'll get it for her. She's not sure what to say about that, so she just takes a sip of her wine and says, "Okay."

At 9:00 sharp, a fleet of cars appear in the front drive. Cate is astounded. She thought they would have to spend the entire weekend going from one dealership to another to test drive cars. She admits that having the cars come to you is pretty cool. After a couple of hours of test driving, Bill asks if she's decided which one she likes best.

She hates to admit it, but she really liked the Volvo best, and the safety rating is very important to her, too. She's just not sure if she can afford it, and she doesn't want him to buy it for her, and she tells him just that. He admits that is exactly what he wants to do, but whatever she decides, he will respect her wishes. He thinks for a minute and suggests that she trade her car in and put down what she had planned, and in a few months after the wedding they'll pay it off.

She knows he's right, but she's still not sure she feels right about it. He tells Kevin they will be in touch later in the day with a decision, and he suggests they go have lunch and give her a little time to think about it.

They drive out to a nice little outdoor café and have salads and walk around to a few little shops in the area. On the drive back home, Cate looks over at Bill and still can't believe what a great guy he is and how quickly she's fallen totally in love with him. He feels her looking at him and glances over and smiles and asks what she's thinking.

Cate answers, "As much as I hate it when you're right, which you usually are, I think you're probably right about the car, too. I know we'll be married in just a couple of months and what you said makes perfect sense--I just don't want you to ever think for a minute that I'm with you for what you can give me. I would never do that."

Bill squeezes her hand. "Baby, I know that. Believe me, I've known a lot of people over the years that want to be my friend, or date me because of what they think they can get from me. I'm not naïve, and I've made a lot of money being able to read people and trusting my instincts. I knew you were not that type of person the first time I met you. Does this mean you're going to let me help you with the car?"

"I'll agree to your last suggestion. I trade in my car, put the down payment, and after we're married, we pay it off.

At least that way I know I'm buying it." He leans over and gives her a quick kiss.

When they get home, Bill calls Kevin and lets him know which car she wants and the color. Kevin says he can get it to them later in the evening. About three hours later, Kevin shows up again in a brand-new, beautiful pearl white Volvo SUV. She signs some papers, gives him her check, and he leaves in her old car.

She never knew that rich people didn't have to go to the dealerships and haggle to buy their cars. This is definitely a perk she could get used to.

After a wonderful night, she wakes up to soft kisses on her neck. She slowly opens her eyes to see Bill's gorgeous face. He says, "Good morning, beautiful."

She smiles and stretches. "Hmmm, good morning."

He's propped up on his elbow looking down at her. "You are so sexy in the morning with your hair all a mess, and those sexy sleepy eyes."

She laughs her deep, sleepy laugh. "Oh yeah, really sexy."

"Yeah, you really are. Girl, you don't know what you do to me. I think I want to continue where we left off earlier this morning."

She laughs again. "You're pretty sexy in the morning, too. Well, you're sexy all the time."

He lies back and pulls her into his arms. "I have a great idea. What if we just spend the whole day right here in bed?"

She lays her head on his chest and cuddles into him and whispers, "Hmmm, as tempting as that is, I could really use some food." She notices the clock on the bedside table. "Oh, my goodness, it's 11:00. We've already stayed in bed all day."

He laughs at her again. "Okay, I guess I can't starve my fiancée. I'll go down and fix something to eat while you shower. That is, unless you'd like some company."

"My goodness, you are insatiable. I may not survive this relationship."

"I'll make sure you survive. Now that I've found you, I'm not letting you go."

Twenty minutes later, she appears in the kitchen smelling more delicious than the omelets and coffee he made for them. He nuzzles her neck and tells her to eat fast, because he's dying for a repeat of last night's adventures. After brunch, he leads her back upstairs, where he says he's ready for his shower and needs her to wash his back.

Later, as they lie out by the pool, Cate can't help thinking, *How did I get so lucky? Bill is so hot and sexy and gorgeous, and if that weren't enough, he's kind and gentle and generous. He's definitely the entire package and he wants to marry me. Go figure.*

Bill comes out of the kitchen with a couple of lemonades for them. "Hey baby, are you daydreaming?"

"Yeah, a little. I was just thinking, in just a few short months this is going to be my home, and I would never have dreamt I'd live in a house like this."

Looking around, he agrees, "You know, growing up I didn't think I would, either. You just never know where life will take you."

She toasts his glass with hers. "I'm glad it took me to you."

"Me too. I've never been happier. You know, we don't have to wait until October. We could fly to Vegas and get married tonight."

She raises her eyebrows. "That sounds like fun, and it would surely take the stress off of planning a wedding, but my mom would kill me and so would yours if we denied them the chance to see us get married. I think we better just stick with the plan."

CHAPTER 42

Monday morning, Cate is really enjoying her drive into work. Her new car is wonderful; it's got so much more room and she loves that new car smell. She smiles as she thinks back over the weekend. *Wow, it's been some weekend. An entirely wonderful, exhausting weekend with my incredible fiancé. A year ago, I thought I'd never see the light at the end of the tunnel. That seems so long ago. Mom kept telling me to just hang in there and pray, and God would see us through. It was so hard to keep the faith at times, but so much has changed so quickly--it makes my head spin. Sometimes I feel guilty for being happy again, but I know Sean would want me to. I can't wait to marry Bill and start our new life.*

Before she knows it, she's turning into the parking lot at Sunrise. She tells herself, *Okay, Cate--time to stop daydreaming and get to work. Even work is entirely different now. I'm actually helping run every aspect of Sunrise Printing. It's really been a great year, and it's only going to get better.*

Hector is getting out of his car when she pulls in. He stops and watches her park and shakes his head. As she gets out he walks up beside her and peeks in the car. "Wow, that's some nice new ride you got there."

She turns to see him almost leaning on top of her to get a better look. "Oh, good morning, Hector. Thanks."

As they walk in the door Hector just can't help thinking how unfair things are. "Wilson, you're not wasting any time, are you?"

Cate walks into her office and sets her purse down on the desk. "What are you talking about?"

"What am I talking about? First the big rock on your hand, now the big expensive new car. I have to say, Wilson, I didn't think you had it in you."

"What? Had what in me? What are you alluding to, Hector?"

He holds up both hands. "Hey look, don't get offended--I don't blame you. If I were a woman and looked like you, I'd use the hell out of it to move myself up in the world, too."

This really hits a nerve. "Don't get offended? I...." She stops herself, knowing the rest of the staff will be coming in. "Would you come into my office for a minute?"

She closes the door and walks behind her desk. "Hector, I don't appreciate you implying that I use my looks, or any other trickery to *hook* Bill or persuade him to buy me things. What goes on in my life, away from work, is none of your business. I do not put my personal life out to anyone at work, nor do I insinuate myself into any of my co-workers' personal lives. I think it would be best if we keep any conversations we have on a purely professional basis."

Hector's shocked she would talk to him like that. Holding up both hands, he says, "Look Cate, I didn't mean any harm. Don't get mad at me if I just say what everyone else is thinking."

"As I said, our conversations from here on out will be work- related only, or I will file a complaint with HR."

"HR-- right. Yeah, no problem, boss lady. Is it okay if I get to work now?"

"That's a good idea. We should both get to work."

After he storms out of her office, she takes a deep breath and says softly to herself, "UGGH! That man makes me crazy."

Just then, Julie gets to her desk right outside of Cate's office. "Hey, good morning, Cate; is that your new car? It's beautiful." Then she notices the look on Cate's face. "Hey, you okay?"

Cate bites her lip. "Oh, yeah—thanks, Julie; I'm fine." She pauses for a minute. "Actually, I *am* fine. I'm going to grab a cup of coffee--you want one?"

Julie's not sure what's going on. "Umm, sure. Thanks."

When Cate gets back with the two cups of coffee, Julie tells her Bill is on line one for her.

She knows she should be really upset from her encounter with Hector, but somehow, she feels just the opposite. She picks up the phone, glad to hear his voice. "Bill, hey. I thought you were on your way to New York."

"Hey, babe, meeting got delayed. I don't leave until this afternoon. How's your morning, beautiful?

She raises her eyebrows. "It's been interesting already."

"Oh? Well, I'm on my way to see you now; you can tell me all about it when I get there."

"You're coming here?"

"Yep. I just need to look into those beautiful big green eyes again."

She laughs. "See you in a few."

About twenty minutes later, Bill walks in. "Good morning, Julie--is she in her office?"

Julie blushes every time Bill talks to her, she thinks he's so good-looking. "Oh, good morning, Mr. Sullivan. Yes, she is."

He walks in and leans over the desk and gives her a kiss. "Hey, babe."

"Hey, I'm so glad to see you again before you leave for the week."

"Is everything okay?"

"It is now. Let me close the door."

As he watches her close the door, he asks, "Okay, what's up?"

She gives him another kiss. "I'm really glad to see you. I had a little discussion with Hector first thing this morning."

This gets his attention. "What happened?"

"Well, he had a comment about the new car, and of course he had to say that I use my looks to move myself up in the world."

Before she can go any further, Bill is on his feet. "WHAT!?"

Cate is surprised; she didn't expect him to be so upset. She stands up, too. "Calm down. I handled it and quite well I think. I told him what goes on in my personal life was none of his business, and that any further conversations we have will be strictly business. I think he was stunned that I stood up to him. I really don't think I'll have any more problems with him."

He turns toward the door. "I'm going to have a talk with him."

Cate rushes around her desk. "No, I told you, I don't want you fighting my battles. I've got this handled."

When she looks in his eyes, they are that same deep blue, almost black, like the night she told him what Selena said. He's furious. "Cate, you're asking me to do something that goes against my very fiber, and it's not just because it's you. I don't tolerate that kind of harassment from any of my employees."

She takes his arm and leads him back to the chair. "Bill, please, I don't want people thinking I run to you every time I have a problem. I've wanted to set him straight for a long time, but couldn't because he was my boss and I needed my job. But now we're on an even level and I don't have to take it anymore. I'm not upset--I actually feel good...empowered."

He looks at her like she's crazy. "Empowered?"

"Yes. Look, I know you want to fix everything for me, and I love that, but you must let me handle my own problems at work. I love you."

He looks at her, and those beautiful green eyes could make him do anything. He calms down a little. "Hmmm. I love you, too. You're killing me, woman. Okay, but I'm telling you, if this happens again, I'm firing him--no questions asked."

She smiles at him, and it's all over; she knows how to make him melt, too. He takes her in his arms and kisses her. He glances at the clock on her wall. "I gotta go, but I'll call you when I get to New York. I wish you were coming with me."

She always feels so good in his arms. "I do too, but I have a really busy week here."

He stops at the door. "Hey, what if you fly up Friday afternoon, and we'll fly back Sunday?"

This piques her interest. "A couple of days in New York with you? Very tempting. Let me see if I can work things out for the girls, and I'll let you know."

He kisses her one more time. "Okay, I gotta run. I love you, babe."

"I love you, too--and thanks for letting me handle things here."

Normally, Bill would have stuck his head into Hector's office to say hi and see how things were going, but he knows today is not the time to talk to Hector. He would not be able to keep his promise to Cate.

Hector sees him drive out of the parking lot and feels uneasy that Bill didn't bother talking to him. It dawns on him that he may have gone too far this time.

CHAPTER 43

The rest of the week goes smoothly. Cate and Hector barely speak, which she's just fine with. She managed to arrange for her neighbor, Beth, to stay with Phoebe and the girls for the weekend. Although she knows Phoebe is now strong enough to handle the girls alone, she just feels better knowing Beth will be there in case it gets to be too much for her mom.

Cate is excited as she leaves work a little early and heads for the airport. Bill told her he's made plans for their weekend, but wouldn't say what they were. She calls him when the plane lands and he says he has a car picking her up, and to look for a guy holding a card with her name.

Cate feels so important when she sees the driver holding up a white card with her last name--this is another first. Bill always thinks of everything. When she arrives at the hotel, he meets her in the lobby; he's excited too and can't wait to get her in his arms.

"Hi, beautiful--thank you for meeting me here. I have a great weekend planned for us."

Seeing him standing in the lobby waiting for her, she still can't believe this gorgeous, wonderful man wants to marry her.

"Ha-ha, I'm sure you do. Did you know that this is my first trip to New York?"

“I didn’t know that. Well, that makes it even more special. Sorry we don’t have more time for me to show you all the sights, but we’ll have to arrange another trip and I’ll show you everything.”

She gives him a sideways glance. “I’d love for you to show me everything.”

This causes him to raise his eyebrows. “Hmmm, you’re being naughty, and we have reservations, but when we get back here tonight, I’ll definitely show you a few things.”

She takes his hand as they head to the elevator to bring her bags up. “Looking forward to it.”

When they get to the room--a penthouse suite, of course—she’s mesmerized at the view of Manhattan. After several minutes, he reminds her they have to get ready to leave to make their dinner reservations. She hates to pull away from the windows, but also can’t wait to see what he has planned. As she heads to the bedroom, she asks what play they are going to see.

Bill reaches in his jacket pocket and pulls out two tickets, holds them up and says, “*Jersey Boys*--hope you haven’t seen it already.”

She laughs. “No, I haven’t, really haven’t seen anything for a while, but I’ve always wanted to see that play. You’re such a wonderful fiancé.”

He reaches for his phone to call for the car to meet them at the door, and as he looks up, he almost forgets who he called. “Wow, you look magnificent! I can’t believe what a lucky man I am.”

She laughs, as she always does when he says stuff like that. “Oh, no--I’m the lucky one to have such a handsome, strong, thoughtful, loving and kind man fall in love with me.”

He pulls her close and breaths in her perfume, as the thought crosses his mind to forget about the plans and just ravish her. But instead he pulls back a little and looks into her sparkling eyes and says, "Seems like we're both pretty lucky."

After a romantic dinner and fabulous box seats for the play, they climb into the back seat of the car to head back to the hotel. Cate is still feeling excited and doesn't want the night to end. She takes Bill's hand and thanks him for a wonderful evening.

"The dinner was great, and the play was awesome--I love that music. I'm so glad you suggested this little weekend get-away."

He squeezes her hand and gives her a little kiss. "Baby, everything I do with you is wonderful. It makes me happy to take you to new places. I love watching your face light up like a little girl's; you amaze me. Tell me what you want to do next--do you want to go out on the town or head back to the hotel?"

She pauses for a moment. "I love both options, but I vote for going back to the hotel; maybe we can do the town tomorrow night."

"Hmmm, that sounds like a plan." He takes her face in his hands and gives her a long, slow kiss. She feels the tingle down to her toes.

Once back in their room, things really heat up. As soon as Bill closes the door behind them, he grabs her hand and spins her around and pins her back against the door. He starts slowly unzipping her dress as he kisses her deeply. All she can do is moan.

They don't even make it to the bedroom; they make love right there on the living room rug. For the next hour, they lie snuggled up together, just enjoying the feel of each other's bodies. Soon Bill's hands start exploring again, and he whispers in her ear for her to come with him to the shower. She just smiles and takes his outstretched hand and lets him lead her.

CHAPTER 44

She wakes the next morning with them still tangled together. She just lies very still and studies his handsome face. Looking at him, she can't believe how deeply in love she is. She suddenly feels the familiar twinge of guilt as Sean crosses her mind. She tries to untangle herself from him without waking him, but he moans, "Don't leave," and pulls her in closer. She lies there silently struggling with her conscience.

A few minutes later, he kisses her neck and asks if she wants to go to breakfast. He finally releases his hold and lets her get up to shower. While in the shower, she allows herself to cry a little. Sometimes her emotions are so confusing. One minute she's on cloud nine, and the next she's beating herself up for being there. She pulls it all together by the time she's finished showering and relinquishes the bathroom to Bill, so he can shower.

As she's putting on her makeup, his phone dings, signaling a text message. She glances over at it, and her heart sinks. It's a message from Selena telling Bill she's glad they got to see each other and looks forward to seeing him again soon.

Just then, Bill comes out of the bathroom with a towel around his waist and asks if there is anything special she wants to see today. When she doesn't answer, he notices she's just standing there staring at his phone. He walks over and asks what's wrong. She just picks up his phone and shoves it into his chest. Confused, he looks at the phone and at her and back at the phone.

He presses the button and the text message lights up. He feels his blood pressure rise as he turns to Cate and says, "This is not what you think."

He tosses the phone on the bed and walks over to Cate as she stands staring out the window. Turning her around, he says, "There is nothing going on between me and Selena. I was out a few nights ago for dinner with my clients and ran into her at the bar as we were waiting for our table. She approached me, and I told her I knew what she tried to pull at the Chamber awards dinner, but it didn't work and that you and I are engaged and getting married in October. Then I walked away and didn't see her again. Cate, I swear I don't know why Selena would send a message like that."

She looks deep into his eyes and wants to believe him, but she just can't understand why Selena would send that message on the off chance that she would see it. That just doesn't make sense, and she tells him so.

He lifts her chin to make her look in his eyes, "This is the happiest I've ever been in my life and I would never do anything to hurt you this way." He reminds her that he didn't want anything to do with Selena when he was unattached, and he sure doesn't want anything to do with her, or any other woman, now. He pleads with her to not let this deranged woman ruin their weekend. All the time his mind is racing to figure out how he's going to make Selena pay for this.

Cate finally says she believes him and doesn't want this to spoil their weekend either. She turns to finish getting ready, but he can tell she's still bothered by it. He suggests after lunch they go for a carriage ride through Central Park.

She just gives a little smile and says that would be nice, without any emotion.

They have lunch at a fancy rooftop restaurant; their table is by a window and he points out some of the famous landmarks to her. Cate is trying her best to forget about the text, but it's still very much on her mind.

After lunch, the carriage ride is beautiful and romantic, and Bill is trying even harder than normal to be attentive. She's not sure if the extra effort is to reassure her, or because he has a guilty conscience, but then she rationalizes that if he was seeing Selena, he probably would not have suggested she come up to New York.

She knows she has a choice to make, either believe him and not let Selena ruin their weekend, or doubt him and fly back home tonight.

As their ride is ending, they both sit quietly, holding hands. She's contemplating her choice and he's in disbelief, wondering why Selena is so dead set on trying to tear them apart and how she would know just when to send that stupid text.

He's saying a silent prayer that Cate knows him well enough to know he would never hurt her that way.

When they get back to the hotel, he opens the door and she walks in before him and stops dead in her tracks. She can't believe what she sees--the entire living room is filled with flowers. She looks around the room then back at him. He just smiles that killer smile and she immediately tears up. How could she have doubted him for even a minute? She throws her arms around his neck and starts to cry and apologizes for thinking he would cheat on her.

Bill whispers in her ear that everything is okay and asks her not to cry. He says, "I understand how it seemed, but you're the one woman I've waited my whole life for, and I'd never hurt you like that." He kisses her and leads her toward the bedroom. He makes love to her slowly and gently, and she knows she can trust him and just wants to stay in his arms forever.

When they emerge from the bedroom, the sun has set over the city and their window is filled with the sparkling lights of New York at night. Bill tells her he wants to take her out on the town, so they shower and dress for the evening.

Bill's wearing a custom-fitted black suit with a baby-blue shirt open at the neck and Cate is wearing a sleeveless black dress that ends slightly above the knee with a slit up the side halfway up her thigh and it fits like a glove. They appreciate the sight of one another and each of them contemplates if they can make it out the door. Cate breaks her stare first, grabs her bag and heads for the door before they can change their minds.

The evening is wonderful; they have dinner and do some club hopping, and a lot of dancing. It's 3 a.m. when they return, and Cate can't remember the last time she was out this late.

Amazingly, Bill speaks her thoughts and says, "Man, it's been a long time since I got home at 3 a.m." She just bursts out laughing and tells him she was just thinking the same thing. They fall together on the couch and look around the flower-filled room and start laughing again.

Cate asks him how he managed to order all the flowers without her knowing, since they were together all day. He laughs and tells her he still has a few tricks up his sleeve. He says, "I ordered them when you went to the bathroom." They both start laughing again.

When the laughter settles down, Cate turns to him and says she has a serious question she's been wanting to ask him. He says he doesn't know if he wants anything serious right now.

She ignores him and says, "What about a pre-nup? I mean, I know someone in your position and all your business interests has to have one to protect your assets. I'm okay with that. I mean, some people see it as planning for your marriage not to work, but I don't. I know how life plans can change in an instant and I want more than anything for you and your family to know that I'm not in this for the money. I love you, and I plan to spend the rest of my life with you, but I also want to be realistic about things."

He blinks and shakes his head. "Wow, okay—well, honestly Ed has been bugging me about working one up, but I don't know. I've been telling him no, because I know you're not in it for the money and the last thing I want is to make you feel like I don't trust you. Cate, I could tell the first day I met you that you were not a gold digger. Believe me, I've known my share."

She smiles, thinking of Selena. "I'm sure you have, but I think it's the smart thing to do. You have all these companies and a lot of people depending on you for their livelihood, so you owe it to them to protect their futures. It's the right business decision, and you know it."

Bill takes her hands. "Well, Ms. Wilson, you make a very compelling argument. I will get with Ed and work something up. You can review it, and we'll make any adjustments you want. Just one more thing we should discuss."

"What's that?"

"I know you're concerned about leaving your mom alone, so I'm having the contractor come in Monday to start construction on remodeling the basement into a separate living suite."

She's again in disbelief of this incredible man. "What? Really? But we don't even know if she'll agree to move yet."

"I know, but I thought if we have it all done she'll see that it will work, and she'll love the space and not be able to say no."

"But what if she still says no, and what are you going to do with all the game room stuff that's in there now?"

"The game room is going to be moved to the pool house. It will probably get more use there anyway, and if she still says no right now, it will be ready in case she changes her mind. I want you to look at the plans tomorrow when we get home and let me know what you think. I also want you to be there Monday to go over everything with the designer. I want it to be what Phoebe would love. I really think you'll like the plans. She'll have her own entrance, her own kitchen and laundry area. She'll never have to see us if she doesn't want to."

Cate starts to tear up again. "I can't believe you're doing this before she even agrees to live with us."

He kisses her. "I just want to make you happy, and I know you will feel better having your mom close. I know how much you worry about her."

She kisses him. "Thank you. I love you."

"I love you, too. Now that we have all that out of the way, let's have some fun."

"What do you have in mind?"

"Well, you know how my mind works--maybe we could make use of that enormous shower in there?"

She raises her eyebrows. "I could use a nice warm shower."

CHAPTER 45

The weeks are flying by, and the basement remodel is almost finished. Cate hasn't mentioned anything to Phoebe yet; she agreed with Bill that it might be harder for her mom to refuse once she sees how beautiful it will be and that they will each have as much privacy as they want.

Ed drew up a very fair pre-nup, and Cate signed it without requesting any changes. She really didn't like the idea of outlining how to divide things up before you are even married, and even though Bill kept telling her she didn't have to sign it at all, she just wouldn't feel right about letting him enter into this marriage without protecting his business.

Things are really falling into place for the wedding, too, thanks to a lot of help from Phoebe, Marjorie, Sherrie, and Cindy. It looks like they will be able to pull off a wedding in three months.

Cate is excited most of the time, but every now and then the guilt grabs her, and she feels like she's betraying Sean. Logically, she knows she's not, but in her heart, she never imagined being with anyone but him, and now she's getting ready to start a new life with someone else.

Phoebe's been making great progress, too. It's a little over a year since her stroke and she's finally feeling like her old self again. Dr. Donaldson gave her the green light to start driving again a few weeks ago, and although she's been keeping her trips short, she loves having her independence. She's been watching Cate and the girls; they've been so happy. Kaylee and Shawn have really blossomed in the last few months. She understands it may be because they are getting a little older, but she believes it also has a lot to do with the loving relationship they see between Cate and Bill.

It's early Saturday morning, and Phoebe is sitting at the kitchen table lost in her own thoughts and watching the hummingbirds buzz back and forth to the feeder hanging on the other side of the window. Cate comes in and pours herself a cup of coffee, sits down, and reaches for her mom's hand. "Good morning, Mom. You look like you were in deep thought--is everything okay?"

Phoebe pats her hand and nods. "Yep, everything is great. I was just thinking how well everything is working out and how happy you and the girls are."

Cate nods in agreement. "It feels good to be happy. It's unbelievable how much my life has changed in such a short time."

Cate pauses for just a moment and glances down into her coffee cup. "Mom, do you really think I'm doing the right thing? I mean, Sean hasn't been gone that long--it seems like just yesterday, and then sometimes it feels like eons. Do you think we're moving too fast? Can you have two loves of your life?"

Phoebe squeezes her hand. "Cate, there is no specified time line on when a person is ready to move on, as you say. God brought Bill into your life at just the right time, when you needed him most. Remember--things don't happen on our timeline, they happen on God's, and I do believe you can have true love more than once in a lifetime. You've got to stop trying to put your happiness on a schedule."

She knows Phoebe is right about the timing, because when Sean died, her life crumbled in an instant, and she thought she would never be whole again. She just doesn't want it to seem like she's forgotten him; he was such a wonderful husband and father.

Phoebe reads the sadness in her daughter's eyes and tells her, "You don't have to stop loving one person to love another. Sean will always be your first love. His time was cut way too short, but he left his legacy behind in Kaylee and Shawn, so part of him will always be with us. Now you have a second chance."

Cate wipes the tears from her eyes. "I know you're right. I'm just so scared that maybe we're rushing into this--and what if it doesn't work out? We've known each other less than a year."

"Oh, baby, it's only natural to be scared and get cold feet, but if I thought for one instant that Bill wasn't the guy for you, I would tell you. You know that. But everything I've seen and come to know about him tells me he's genuine, and watching the two of you together, it's plain to see you're meant for each other. Now you can second-guess it and run away, but I think that would be a big mistake."

"Mom, how can I be so sure one minute and so confused the next?"

Phoebe gets up and hugs her. "It's only natural to be scared. You just said how happy you are--allow yourself to enjoy your happiness."

Cate waits until her mom sits down again before telling her, "You know the other day when I went to the cemetery, I think I may have gotten a sign from Sean."

Phoebe stops with the coffee cup halfway to her mouth. "Oh?"

Cate explains, "I was talking to Sean and telling him about my plans to marry Bill and asking him if he was okay with it, and suddenly, a butterfly landed on his headstone and just sat there fanning its wings."

Cate pauses for a couple of seconds to swallow hard, so she can continue taking over the lump in her throat. "Sean used to say that butterflies reminded him of new beginnings. You know the whole caterpillar into a butterfly thing. Do you think Sean was sending his approval?" She shrugs her shoulders. "I don't know, that's what I thought. I just hope Sean doesn't think I've forgotten him already."

Phoebe grabs a couple of tissues for each of them before answering, "Sean knows you haven't forgotten him. I believe when you get to the other side, you're able to see the bigger picture and you know people's true feelings and thoughts. I think you lose that human pride that makes us see things from a 'me' perspective, and you can see that love is all we really have.

"I believe we do get signs from our loved ones on the other side, if we just pay attention. Sometimes I feel like your dad's here with me--and then I might come across something of his and wonder if he was really here and left it for me to find."

Cate reflects on that thought for a minute, then nods. "I think Sean would have liked Bill."

"I do too. I think Sean would be happy that you and the girls have found such a great guy to love and take care of you."

This time, Cate gets up and hugs her mom. "Thank you, Mom; you're my best friend."

CHAPTER 46

Bill's been busy, too. He promised Cate he wouldn't dump all the work of planning the wedding on her, and he hasn't. Although he is cheating a little by enlisting Laura's help, he's still getting it done.

He's been contemplating a wedding gift for Cate, so he met with Ed and outlined what he wants. Of course, Ed advised against it, but he's worked with Bill long enough to know once he's got his mind set on something, it's not easy to sway him.

Ed brings in the contracts for Bill to review, and they go over it together page by page. He likes it, but asks for a few tweaks. He can't wait to see Cate's face when he gives her full control of Sunrise Printing as a wedding present.

Although it will stay under Sullivan Enterprises umbrella, she will call the shots, and if for some reason things didn't work out between them, she would own Sunrise free and clear. He's also had Ed revise his will to go into effect on the day after their wedding, giving Cate full control of Sullivan Enterprises should anything happen to him. Bill thought Ed was going into cardiac arrest when he first told him of his plans, but Bill has absolutely no doubts or fears. He knows Cate is the woman he's waited his whole life for, and after working closely with her for almost a year, he knows she's very capable of taking the reins should something happen.

Although it's only three more weeks until the wedding, October 17th can't get here soon enough for him. Bill tried to convince Cate to have a huge wedding at one of the most exclusive venues in Charleston, but she just couldn't see spending that kind of money. And even though he keeps telling her they can afford whatever she wants, she's just not into overindulgence. So, they decided to exchange their vows in the gazebo at Bill's house, with the reception to follow there on the grounds. Bill wanted to invite everyone he's ever known, but Cate wanted to keep it to just family and close friends.

Of course, Bill did have to include his closest employees and a few long-time business associates, and he insisted she invite all the Sunrise Printing employees. Neither of them was thrilled about inviting Hector, but they did. Things between Cate and Hector have leveled off; they speak to each other only regarding business, but she can tell he really resents her, and several of the other long-term employees have let her know he still passes snide remarks about her. But she's chosen to ignore that and hopes he will one day find something new to obsess about.

Cate and Bill finally agreed to a cut-off of 200 people, much more than Cate wanted, but it's amazing how quickly the count adds up. Bill had Laura book a great local band, and he was in charge of getting the tents. They are hoping for good weather, but want the tents ready just in case.

He also volunteered to plan the honeymoon; he wants to surprise her with a family trip to Hawaii. He just loves the idea of finally having his own family, and he adores Kaylee and Shawn.

TJ will be Bill's best man, and Cindy is going to be Cate's matron of honor. They've picked out the wedding bands, cake, glasses, flowers, photographer, and all the other things that women think you need for a wedding.

Bill's only concern now is Cate. He sees the way she sometimes gets quiet and tells him nothing's wrong, but he knows she's still torn between mourning for Sean and allowing herself to be happy. He can't say he knows how she feels, but he does understand. He just wants to fill the rest of her life with love and happiness.

He's even thought about asking to adopt the girls, but thinks it best to wait a while and let Cate get comfortable with their new life. The last thing he wants is for her to think he's trying to wipe Sean out of their lives.

CHAPTER 47

It's October 10th, one week before the wedding, and it's Cate's birthday. She just wants a quiet family dinner at Bill's house with Phoebe and the girls. They will have cake Sunday at Ted and Marjorie's with the Sullivan crew. Construction is finally finished on the basement, and it turned out better than Cate thought it would. After dinner they plan to show Phoebe the new basement space and ask her to move in after the wedding. Cate is hoping she will agree.

Over dinner, Phoebe expresses how excited she is to be driving again and to not have to depend on everyone else to bring her places. She turns to Cate and says she knows it will take a lot of burden off her.

Cate shakes her head. "Mom, it's no burden. I don't mind at all bringing you wherever you have to go. After all you did it for me for about--I don't know, eighteen years, or so--and still do."

Phoebe laughs. "True, but you were a kid and couldn't drive for most of those years."

"Doesn't matter; you still did it. By the way, Bill and I have something we want to show you. Bill had some remodeling done in the basement."

Phoebe's surprised. "Oh, I can't imagine what you would want to change in this perfect house."

Before they get up from the table, Bill hands Cate a pretty baby-blue box and tells her happy birthday. He doesn't understand why she looks surprised--did she think he wasn't going to get her a present? She looks at her mom with her eyes sparkling like a child's; when she opens the box, her mouth drops open. All she can say is, "Oh, Bill." She turns the box so Phoebe can see; it's a beautiful emerald and diamond necklace, very dainty and elegant. Bill takes the box, removes the necklace, and puts it on Cate's neck.

Phoebe puts her hands to her mouth. "Oh, Cate, it's just beautiful; you should wear it for the wedding."

Cate reaches up and brushes her fingers over the necklace as tears start to form in her eyes. Bill kisses her and suggests they go show Phoebe the basement before the waterworks start. They all get up from the table and start toward the basement. Cate can't stop touching the necklace.

When they reach the bottom of the stairs, Phoebe is shocked at the difference. "Wow, you've moved all the game stuff out. This is beautiful, but why the change?"

They look at each other and Bill says, "Well, we were hoping you would like it enough to agree to move in here after the wedding."

"What? You did this for me?"

"Yes. We hope you like it."

"It's beautiful, but I can't move in here with you two newlyweds. My Lord, I would feel like such a third wheel. Besides, I have a house. What would I do with my house?"

Bill puts his arm around her shoulder as he walks her through the apartment and shows her everything. "Phoebe, you would not be a third wheel. We really want you here--both of us want you here. Look, we've made this space entirely separate; you have your own entrance, your own kitchen, bath, and laundry. It's a whole independent living area, so you don't even have to see us if you don't want to. Besides, having you here would be great for the girls. I know they would miss you like crazy, all three of them."

Cate chimes in, "Mom, please at least think about it. You could sell the house and use that money to do the traveling that you and Aunt Alison always talked about. We would not be in each other's way at all."

Phoebe looks around the beautiful apartment and sighs. "Cate, I don't know, I just don't know. I'll have to think about this."

Bill doesn't want Phoebe to feel pressured, so he says, "Okay, no pressure. It's your decision, but it's here for you if you want it."

She looks around again in disbelief. "I appreciate it, but I'll have to think about it."

Phoebe never dreamt of leaving her home, but the apartment is beautiful, and she knows she'll miss Cate and the girls like crazy. Over the next few days she debates the pros and cons, and realizes the basement apartment is a great solution, Phoebe decides she will move in with Bill and Cate, but she insists they wait six months, to give the newlyweds time to adjust to their new life.

CHAPTER 48

The next week goes by in a blink of an eye and suddenly, it's October 17th, the wedding day. Cate's been awake since 2 a.m., pacing her bedroom. Her mind has been racing all over the place. One minute she is so thrilled to have found Bill and wants nothing more than to marry him, then the next she's scared to death that this all happened too fast and it won't work out.

She knows she loves being with him, but is it love that will last? Marrying Bill will ensure she and the girls never have any financial worries again, but she can't marry someone just for security. She stops herself, thinking she would still love being with him if he was just an ordinary guy with a 9-5 job, living from paycheck to paycheck. So that argument is off the table.

She looks at her ring and walks over to where her wedding dress is hanging. She brushes her fingers lightly over the dress and starts to cry.

Bill's been up most of the night, too, but he's not questioning the marriage; he's so excited he just couldn't sleep. His dream of a life filled with love and a family of his own is finally coming true. He truly thought it just wasn't meant for him, but in just a few hours it will all be reality.

The wedding is set for 11 a.m., so by 6 a.m. the house starts bustling. The reception tent was erected yesterday. This morning the workers are setting up the tables and chairs, the bandstand and the dance floor in there. The caterers are busy setting up the buffet tables, and the food will be arriving soon. There are more workers setting up the chairs in front of the gazebo, which is being decorated with a variety of beautiful white flowers.

By 8 a.m. the hair and makeup lady arrives at Cate's house to get Cate, Cindy, Phoebe, Kaylee, and Shawn prettied up. Cate's still pacing struggling with her conflicting thoughts. She asks the hairdresser to start with Phoebe and Cindy first. She tells them she'll be right back, she has something she has to do, as she rushes toward the door.

Cindy turns to Phoebe and asks if she thinks Cate is okay. Phoebe shakes her head yes, and says she's just nervous, but silently she's wondering if Cate is running.

Bill's mom and dad showed up early, so they could oversee the set-up. Marjorie is just brimming with happiness to finally see Bill so happy. They are all so thrilled he found such a wonderful woman; they've all come to love Cate and her girls. It's like they've always been a part of the family.

Marjorie finds Bill in his bedroom; he's already showered and shaved and is debating whether it's too early to start getting dressed. She knocks on his open door before entering. Bill turns to see his mom and tells her to come in. She closes the door behind her, so she can have a private minute with him before everyone else gets there.

"Well, son, this is it--your wedding day."

He hugs his mom. "I know. Never thought you'd see it, did you, Mom?"

"Well, I was starting to wonder, but I'm glad you waited. Cate is a wonderful girl, and I've never seen you happier."

"I guess sometimes I wondered if it would ever happen, too. I knew love existed, but I thought maybe it wasn't in the cards for me. I never really believed in that love at first sight stuff until that day one year ago today when I met my future."

Marjorie starts to tear up. "Honey, I'm so happy for you. Look at you, becoming a husband and a father all in one day."

"Mom, I really want to be a good dad to those kids. They've been through so much. All I want is to make them happy, all of them."

"Oh, you will be a wonderful dad. It's plain to see you love them, and they just adore you. I was a little worried at first, though. I mean, I know you love kids, but I didn't know how you would handle an immediate family. I have to say, I'm very impressed at how quickly you've adjusted."

"You know, from the moment I saw Cate, I knew she was the one, and it was just natural that it would be a family, not just the woman I'd been waiting for."

She kisses his cheek. "Your dad and I have always been proud of all of you, but it still amazes me to see the man you've become. You've accomplished so much, yet you're still the same person you've always been."

Suddenly, there's a frantic knocking at the door.

CHAPTER 49

He hears Cate's voice call his name and knock again. As he moves to open the door he calls back, "Cate, is that you?"

"Yes, Bill, I need to talk to you."

Marjorie says, "Wait, you're not supposed to see the bride before the wedding."

"I think it's okay, Mom. She sounds like something's wrong." He pulls the door open. "Cate, baby, what's the matter?"

She looks frantic. "Bill, I have to talk to you." Bill looks at Marjorie. "Mom, will you excuse us please?"

Marjorie is stunned, but says of course, and that she'll go check on the caterer.

Bill grabs Cate's hands. "Honey, what's wrong? Is everyone okay?"

"Yes, everyone is fine. Except me, that is."

As Cate paces the floor, Bill becomes worried.

"Bill, I...I just don't know if I can do this. I mean...I love you, but what if we're rushing things? I mean...the girls. Bill, what about them?"

"Okay, first--breathe, calm down, and let's talk." Bill's getting nervous now, too. "Cate, if this is too soon and you want to postpone, we will. Look, I know I pushed for a quick wedding. I just want us to be a family so bad. I don't want to push you into something you're not ready for. We can postpone, a few months, a year, whatever you want--just don't walk away from us."

She's still pacing. "Oh, God--what's wrong with me? I have the most wonderful guy in the world, and I'm afraid to marry him. I don't want to walk away from us; I'm just having a panic attack."

Bill takes her hand again and leads her to a chair by the window. "Okay, here--drink a little water, and come sit here with me. Let me just hold you; then we can talk this out."

She looks at him with that deer in the headlights look, and finally starts to move toward the chair. "Okay, I'm sorry."

"Don't be sorry. Baby, I love you, and if you want to wait, we'll wait."

"I don't know if I want to wait. I don't know what I want, or what's wrong with me."

He hugs her tight. "This is my fault--maybe I pushed too hard. Cate, I never meant to push you into doing something you're not ready to do. If you want to postpone, we will, and I'll contact everyone and explain we had a family emergency and have to delay the wedding. Don't misunderstand; this is not what I want, but I'll wait as long as I have to for you. I'm not going anywhere. Hell, it took me too long to find you." He lifts her chin, to take her gaze from her hands. "Are you okay?"

Looking into his eyes, she takes a deep breath. "I'm better. I'm so sorry; I know I was a lunatic when I first got here. Are you sure you want to marry a crazy woman? Oh, good Lord, your mother must think I've lost my mind."

He laughs. "I'm positive I want to marry *this* crazy woman, and don't worry about my mom. She loves you, too. Tell me what you want to do."

Cate shakes her head. "Whew! I just don't know."

Bill waits a beat, then squeezes her hand. "Look, how about this? You go back home and think things through. If you decide you want to postpone, you call me, and I'll take care of everything. If you don't call, I'll be waiting for you at the altar."

Cate looks at him and starts to cry. "Oh, Bill."

He just pulls her close. "Sssh, it's okay. We have a few hours before wedding time. Now just clam down and think it through. If at any time you decide you can't do this right now--I don't care if it's five minutes before you walk down the aisle--just call me. I'll have my phone on me the whole time. I love you, Cate. I want to marry you today, but I'll wait if that's what you want. I just can't be without you."

She wipes her tears. "I love you, too. I don't know why I'm so scared. Thank you for being so patient and understanding with me. My mom and Cindy must think I'm crazy. I just left them and Aunt Alison with the girls and the make-up and hair lady at the house. Good Lord, I really have lost my mind."

He kisses her gently. "That's okay. I like crazy."

This makes her laugh. "Good thing. Okay, I'm going home now. I'm sorry."

Hugging her tightly against him, he kisses her hair and whispers in her ear, "No sorrys."

CHAPTER 50

Marjorie catches a glimpse of Cate's car driving down the driveway and goes inside to check on Bill. She goes back to his bedroom and finds him there looking out the window, watching her drive away. "Is everything okay?"

Without turning, he says, "Mom, I think I pushed too hard. I should have known better than to rush her, knowing all she's been through."

"Is Cate calling off the wedding?"

"No—well, I hope not. She had a panic attack, and I don't know--I told her to just calmly think things through and if she wants to postpone, we will. I should just be glad to have her and the girls in my life. Mom, I hope I didn't push too hard. I can't lose her."

She walks over and hugs her son. "Oh, honey, just tell me what I can do."

He hugs her back. "Just don't say anything to anyone about this. I'm hoping once she calms down, she'll meet me at that altar. No one else has to know there was ever an issue. Please."

"Okay--no one will ever hear it from me."

"Thanks, Mom. I'm going to finish getting ready now." When his mother leaves the room, he sits on the bed with his head in his hands thinking, *Come on Cate, please meet me at that altar.*

CHAPTER 51

Wedding time is fifteen minutes away and still no word from Cate. As Bill waits with his dad and TJ he thinks, *No news is good news.* He doesn't know if he's more nervous about getting married or about the possibility of not getting married. Now he paces, thinking, *Come on, baby, don't back out on me.* Sherrie pokes her head in the door and tells them it's time to start to the gazebo. Bill nods, thinking, *Okay, here goes--please come to me, Cate.*

As they walk toward the gazebo, Bill sees his mom and motions her over. "Mom, is she here yet?"

"Not yet, but I know she'll show. If she hasn't called you by now, I'm sure she won't stand you up."

"I hope not. Love you, Mom."

"Love you, too."

Bill and TJ enter the gazebo and shake hands with the minister. Bill looks out at all the guests and thinks, *Man, I've stood before hundreds of strangers and made presentations and speeches and never felt as nervous as I do right now standing in front of a group of family and friends praying Cate shows up.*

Suddenly the music starts, and he hopes that means she's here.

Bill lets out a big sigh of relief as he sees Cindy start up the aisle followed by Kaylee and Shawn, each with a little baket of white rose petals. As they spread the petals on the ground, Cate appears like an angel under the arch of flowers. He smiles so big it hurts his face, but he just can't stop smiling as he watches her walk up the path of rose petals toward the gazebo.

When she reaches him, and takes his hand, he says, "Oh Cate, you're so beautiful--I love you. I will make you happy, and we will be together forever, I promise."

She smiles and says, "I love you, too. Let's do this." Out of the corner of her eye, she sees a beautiful butterfly flutter by and disappear into the trees.

CPSIA information can be obtained
at www.ICGtesting.com
Printed in the USA
FSHW02n2028210618
49585FS